SOLITAIRE

An Adam Fraley Mystery

HENRY HOFFMAN

My gratitude goes to Barbara Whelehan for her assistance in the preparation of the manuscript.

"I myself am best when least in company."

— WILLIAM SHAKESPEARE, TWELFTH
NIGHT

PROLOGUE

May 1997

LIGHT ATTRACTS. NOTHING EXTRAORDINARY ABOUT THAT WHEN considering creatures of every species. For Jeb Lanigan, it was the source of the light that ultimately would land him at the epicenter of a great American tragedy.

Back in the seventies, Jeb would take a round-trip train ride once every summer from his hometown of Reno, Nevada, to San Francisco to visit his grandmother who had retired to San Jose across the Bay. He adored his grandmother, but in all honesty, it was the train rides that spurred him westward. Jeb was a man filled by wanderlust, and the cross-country treks were a convenient way of satiating some of that lust.

As an independent financial advisor who was already approaching burned-out status at the age of forty, he recently had considered jumping off the grid. At first, he fell for the attractions of his profession—the chance to offer meaningful advice on one of the more important aspects of a person's life, the opportunity for him to be his own boss, the prospect of unlimited earning potential, not to mention the flexible hours. Altogether, it amounted to a comfortable lifestyle for one who harbors no desire to further climb the ladder of success. It wasn't long, though, before the cons came to the fore, especially the one when you come to realize that you are, in fact, taking on a heavy responsibility in handling other people's money and not always to their satisfaction. The flexible hours were turning into a daily twenty-four-hour grind. How many times had he advised a client to invest in a certain stock, and when the issue dropped a fraction of a point, the client called him immediately on the phone the next day questioning the decision? As for other responsibilities, he had few. He was single—never married—an only child whose parents were independently wealthy and, unlike his grandmother, a thousand miles away, much more into their lives than his.

"Face it, you're devoting all your time to the lives of others, not your own," he told himself while on one of his trips to see his granny. *"Time for a mid-course correction, before it's too late."* That's when he saw the light, quite literally.

Gazing out over a darkened landscape from the window of his Amtrak cabin, he could vaguely make out the outline of the Sierra Nevada mountains as the train approached the California border just past Verdi, Nevada. For miles on end, pine trees and hills cloaked in shadows lulled him into a meditative state, until he saw that light off in the distance.

He soon realized it was a cluster of lights he was viewing, indicating a remote human presence of some sort. A homestead? A tiny village? A roadside tavern? From what he could discern, the source of the distant light was coming from the slopes of the Sierra foothills, perhaps twenty to thirty miles inland. Rough terrain for any kind of commercial enterprise, he surmised. He had often seen similar sightings in his rail travels, invariably leading him to ponder the strong attraction such isolated places held for him...calling him, like a lost soul in the night.

One of the lights, he noted, shone substantially larger than the others and emitted almost a strobe effect, as if calling attention to the locale. Then, slowly, the lights faded from view as the train continued on its way. Before they had dimmed completely, Jeb had made up his mind to revisit them on his return trip, the next time up close and personally.

CHAPTER ONE

August 1997

ADAM FRALEY WALKED INTO HIS OFFICE AND EXHALED A DEEP breath. "Hot one out there."

"A man who said he was a former client of yours stopped in to see you, Adam," his office manager said in greeting him from across the room, her eyes remaining fixed on her computer.

He dropped his briefcase aside his desk and his backside on a swivel chair, wheeling it in her direction. "Did you recognize him?"

"Nope."

"Did he give a name?"

"Nope."

"Did he flash lethal malice in his eyes?"

"No, but his eyes were bright green to go with his red hair. Ring a bell?"

Adam pondered it a moment. "Can't say it does. Must be a client dating back to when my old boss Pete Peterson was running the show."

"The good old days, as you so often remind me."

Adam let the lighthearted barb fly by.

"He said he would drop back in, as soon as he finished running an errand," she added.

No sooner had she mentioned it than the front door to the office swung open and in stepped the red-haired guy with the green eyes, clad in a blue shirt and tan trousers, and carrying a briefcase.

Adam chided himself. The red hair should have been enough of a clue. "Cal Taylor! What brings you to town?"

"Regional sales meeting."

Adam motioned for him to have a chair. "You still in the gaming business?"

"Yep. It's growing too fast to jump off what with all the Indian casinos opening up. And it's only going to get bigger."

"Not surprising, considering all the employee background checks we were doing for you back in the day. You brought us a lot of business."

"This place doesn't look all that different from when I last saw it," Cal observed, before landing his eyes on the striking woman sitting across from them.

"Cal, I'd like for you to meet my wife, Tamra," Adam said, picking up on the one obvious difference noted by his former client.

Tamra momentarily lifted her gaze from the computer screen to exchange nods and soft smiles with the walk-in.

Cal glanced back at Adam, as if to say, "How did *you* rate?"

"How's business for you?" he asked instead.

"The world is never going to run out of cheating spouses or employees," Adam pointed out, "not to mention missing persons. They are considered renewable resources in this business."

"Funny, you should mention missing persons. It is my primary reason for being here."

"Oh, yeah?" Adam responded in surprise.

"Yes, a longtime friend of mine has gone missing. His name is Jeb Lanigan. He was the best man at my wedding, Adam, and a former college roommate."

"He lives here in Tampa?" Adam asked.

"No, he lives in Reno, Nevada, though I can't be sure about that at the moment. We've stayed in close touch through the years and have frequently visited each other, oftentimes on business-related matters. My job has taken me to Reno on a number of occasions for national gaming seminars."

"His occupation is?"

"Independent financial advisor."

"And he's now missing?"

"It appears so. I have not been able to reach him in several months, which is very unusual."

"Does he have a workplace?"

"He works out of his home."

"His clients must be missing him also," Adam jibed.

"He did mention to me at one time that he had a buyer-in-wait to take over his business in case he ever decided to pack up and leave."

"To go where?"

"Off the grid," Cal said directly.

"You mean to go it alone in the wilds?"

"Maybe not so much off the grid as off the beaten path. Jeb loved taking train rides for that very reason. At night he'd sit up in the dome car and spot these small clusters of lights off in the distance and wonder what they represented. A tiny community? A homestead? An isolated tavern? He was always tempted to hop off the train, rent a car and go find out what exactly it was he was seeing."

"On the chance it would lead him to a better life," Adam opined.

"Yes. 'Count me among those who believe they were born 200 years too late,' he would say."

"Like there was no need for financial advisors back then?" Adam responded, recognizing too late the flippancy of his comment.

"That's not the point, Adam," his office manager interjected from across the room.

"Okay, dear, tell me what is the point," he said, still annoyed with himself for his previous remark.

"The point is there was a lot less intensity in society back in those days."

Adam raised his hands halfway into the air in mock surrender mode and returned his attention to Taylor, who bore a grin on his face, following the interplay. "As you were saying..."

Taylor continued. "When he related his travel experiences to me, particularly his attraction to faraway places, I never felt he'd actually follow through on one of his impulses to the extent he would pull the plug on what appeared to be a lucrative lifestyle. I figured they were pipe dreams."

"And now you think he may have."

Cal nodded. "The last time I spoke with him, he was telling me about his most recent sighting. Jeb, on occasion, would take the train from Reno to San Francisco to visit his grandmother, whom he considers his sole remaining relative since he became estranged from his parents. On his most recent ride there, he spotted a cluster of lights coming from the foothills of the Sierra Nevada mountains near Verdi, Nevada, which is close to the California border. Apparently, they were alluring enough for him to succumb to temptation, as he outright declared he was ready to follow through on that lingering urge of his and check them out. That was the last time I heard from him."

"Did you contact the buyer of his business? Or, am I wrong in assuming he sold it?"

"I did. They have no idea where he is now. It looks like he got all of his affairs in order, sold his house, and ended all of his contracts...phone...electricity...anything that could be tied to his old identity. And I'm sure Jeb was smart enough not to leave any outstanding debts. I understand it's rule number one for people planning to disappear. Debt collectors will never stop looking for you."

"If anyone should know about the importance of paying off debt, it would be a financial advisor—someone familiar with risk," Adam said. "Did you contact the Nevada cops about your friend?"

"Yes, and they showed no interest in chasing after a grown man who was in no apparent peril."

"Standard reply in these situations. What about private eyes out that way?"

"Correct me if I'm wrong, Adam, but I see the personal element as the most appealing part of your profession. I call a P.I. firm out west and I'm likely to get a regional or statewide outfit that will subcontract it out. Local, small, and personal...that's what I'm looking for...all expenses paid."

Adam thought a moment. The offer was on the table and it wasn't the gaming kind...or was it?

"How good of a friend is he to you, Cal? A friend to the end?"

"A friend to the end, for sure," he replied. "I'll put it this way. When it comes to listing personal references on my resumes, he's always at the top of the list. Or, to put it another way...If I happened to be the one to go missing, he would be the first to come looking for me...that is, if he wasn't missing in the first place."

"*Which begs the question, 'How often does one missing person go looking after another missing person?'*" Adam mused. "What make of vehicle did he drive? He may have gotten rid of everything, but he still needed one to get him to wherever he was headed."

"For as long as I've known Jeb, he's always driven pickups, though recently he'd been considering trading it in for a van, perhaps to live out of in case he did decide to take off," Taylor explained. "I wish I could give you more clues to his whereabouts, but he didn't leave many footprints."

"The true off-the-grid guys seldom do." Adam opined.

He glanced at his wife across the way, a nettled smile fixed on her face as she began to sort through the mail. The reason for it, he would soon hear.

"Based on my previous experiences, Cal, I can tell you what a week's worth of my time will buy you. One, whether he is alive and well. Two, whether he is alive and in danger, in which case I call the cops. Three, I don't find any trace of him at all, in which case you would have to hire a local private eye out there to carry on the search. Four, that he is deceased for whatever reason."

"It's a deal, Adam."

"Okay...I'll need a photo of him and any other personal information you might have—phone numbers, addresses, doctors or dentists of his, even if they are no longer in play."

Cal reached down and patted his briefcase. "I have it all right here," he said.

———

ADAM WALKED ACROSS THE ROOM, planted his hands on his wife's desk, and leaned in to address her. "A lot less intensity back then?"

"Definitely," she said, running her hand through her lush auburn hair while keeping her gaze glued to the computer screen she was scanning. "Society wasn't as tightly wired as it is today."

"Tell me—how much more intense can a place get when a substantial portion of the population west of the Mississippi is walking around in those days with a gun strapped to their side, all the while trying to decide whether they liked your face enough, so as not to shoot you?"

Tamra looked at him and widened her eyes like he might want to reconsider his response.

"Not your face, of course," he immediately backtracked. "If everyone out west back then had a face as appealing as yours, there would have been nothing but peace and tranquility throughout the region. There would have been no need for sheriffs."

"Adam, let it go—get back to the case at hand," she smartly stated.

"Sure—what's your opinion of it?"

"My opinion is more of an observation. It's that you've accepted the case."

"And I shouldn't have? He was a very loyal customer of ours and sent a load of business our way back when Pete and I were struggling to keep this operation afloat."

Tamra set aside the stack of mail she had begun to sort to give him full attention. "I understand, but aren't you forgetting something?"

"What's that?"

"You and I are scheduled to take Noelle on college visits two weeks from today."

He smacked his forehead. "Oh. God, I did forget...oh man...is there any chance you could..."

"Adam, she's going to be very disappointed if you don't come along," she said, squashing the suggestion midstream. "She will want your impressions as much as mine."

"I thought we decided not to be hovering over her activities. Helicoptering...isn't that what they call it nowadays?"

"Helping our daughter check out colleges is not helicoptering, Adam. It's supporting."

"You're right," he sighed, "though I wonder why a girl who is only halfway through high school needs to be looking that far ahead."

"Unlike her father, she plans ahead."

"Interesting, how she now wants me to accompany her on these college visits. What a change from the times I have driven her to and from school when she was terrified that I would somehow embarrass her in front of her classmates." Adam chuckled. "Remember the day I was scheduled to pick her up after class and faked having a flat tire in the school parking lot?" he asked. "I had the car all jacked up and the tire off when all her friends started piling out. To make matters worse, I asked her boyfriend at the time if he would help fix it."

"How could I not remember? It's a good thing her boyfriend was in on it at the time or you would never have heard the end of it."

"You have to admit it was funny."

"If you say so," she replied, smothering a smile.

"Whatever happened to that kid? He was one of the few suitors of hers I liked."

"I believe she lost interest in him."

"Of course, when I start liking them, she loses interest."

"If you're looking for sympathy, you're not getting it from me."

"I think it's a good idea to get a dose of humility early in life," he continued. "Sometimes I think how nice it would be to have a daughter who was a little less intelligent—you know, someone who wouldn't be machine-gunning me with all these probing questions of hers all day long."

Tamra grinned. "You always seem to come up with the answers."

"Self-preservation," he lamented, before returning his attention to the matter at hand. "So, that gives me a two-week deadline, unless I fly back to do the college tour and then return to the case."

"Our caseload is locked in for the remainder of the summer, Adam. There is very little wiggle room left."

"Okay, we'll be ready to do the college campus tour in two weeks," he said, issuing his stamp of approval. "Can you do a public records search on this guy Jeb Lanigan? Meanwhile, I'll book a flight to Reno."

"Considering all the long-distance work we have been doing recently, maybe I should come up with a new business card for us, featuring a slogan like...' 'Have magnifying glass—will travel,' along with a cute little Sherlock Holmes caricature inscribed on it."

He again planted his hands on her desk and leaned into her deep green eyes, whispering to her, "You should know by now, Tamra, there is nothing remotely cute about this business—other than the office manager."

"Adam!"

CHAPTER TWO

THE FOLLOWING AFTERNOON, ADAM LANDED IN RENO, RENTED A Jeep, and booked a room at a downtown hotel for the following night. He spent the remainder of the day studying a railway guide and a map of Western Nevada, before heading out on his search. He had reserved a roundtrip Amtrak coach seat from Reno to Truckee, California, a short distance across the border. He had first considered driving the route but figured he would follow Jeb Lanigan's path since it likely would provide him a better vantage point to view the cluster of lights Cal was referencing. He planned to find a place to stay the night in Truckee.

In time, he was riding the rails, heading westward. To give himself an even better view, he moved to the dome car after a stop in Verdi, Nevada. Unlike a kid with his head pressed against the window watching everything from farms to mountains go by, he instead focused on the shadowy Sierra foothills outlined against a darkening sky. He knew he had only one real shot at seeing what Jeb Lanigan saw. Due to time constraints, he wasn't about to take multiple trips back and forth in case he missed the vision on his first pass-by. Besides, was it really a vision Jeb had witnessed or simply an illusion?

He felt the train rumble across a trestle. According to the maps, the route they were following ran parallel to the I-80 Interstate Highway and Truckee River, both of which he caught glimpses of as the train rocked along.

Minutes whisked by as fast as power line polls. By now, they had to be close to the California border or even across it. His conjecture regarding an illusion was rapidly gaining credence with him when, all of a sudden, Lanigan's lights made an appearance off in the distance. Three of them to be precise...one larger than the other two was about all he could discern by the time they floated out of view. Tough to say how far away they were. Nonetheless, he had found his starting point.

Adam departed the train at Truckee. On the ride in, he spotted a cheap motel within walking distance of the station to spend the night. In the morning, he took the eastbound train back to Reno. On his return trek, he had daylight to assist him in his surveillance of the land along the way. He observed carefully the setting in the area where he first spotted the lights. As expected, running parallel to the railroad tracks along this stretch was the Truckee River and the I-80 Interstate Highway. A dirt access road in turn ran between the tracks and the bordering hillsides. He particularly recalled the trestle the train crossed over minutes before his sighting of the lights.

After checking into the hotel he previously booked, Adam phoned Tamra to inform her of his discovery. In return, she informed him she had yet to turn up anything out of the ordinary in her public records search on Lanigan that might help with the case but would keep at it.

"So, you're headed out to the mountains," she said with a hint of concern in her voice. "Just don't fall off of one, Adam."

He laughed. "These are foothills, Tamra, though to us Floridians they may seem like mountains."

Since it was still early in the day, he grabbed several bottles of water and snacks he purchased from the hotel restaurant, tossed them into the Jeep, and headed out to continue his search. Less than an hour later, having navigated Reno traffic, he took a side road over to the dirt trail paralleling the rail line. Shortly, he crossed over the culvert, at which point he scanned the slopes for pathways into the foothills. A trail map would have come in handy at this juncture in his journey, but he had none. Instead, he kept an eye out for ruts, possibly the result of motor vehicle activity or foot traffic.

The first inklings of a pathway had him turning onto the supposed trail, only to discover it was a case of mistaken identity on his part when he hit a dead end a half-mile up the slope. Hurriedly, he turned the Jeep around and headed back down the hill to the dirt access road. He took a minute to gather his bearings, noting the location of the train trestle from where he currently sat and the point past the bridge where he most likely saw the light. If there was a pathway, its entrance had to be close by, he determined, so he soldiered on. Roughly fifty yards further along, his judgment was confirmed, as the semblance of a trail came into view. He quickly swung the Jeep onto the path, confident he was traveling the right course.

The path took him on a slow climb. It was a narrow, weed-strewn, occasionally rocky road, sections of which had his vehicle bouncing like a buckboard. At one point, he was forced to stop and drag away a large fallen tree limb that blocked his path. Nonetheless, it was a beautiful day, with the hills awash in bright sunshine and the distinct scent of pine trees infusing the air.

He glanced at the mileage gauge. He was approaching the thirty-mile mark since first launching his trek up the slope. Despite the rough going and the occasionally lateral path he was taking, he had to have reached over two thousand feet in elevation, he figured. No sooner had doubt crept back into his mind as to whether he had chosen the correct route, when he rounded a curve and entered a spacious, leveled clearing, bringing into view the first sign of a human presence, since beginning his climb. Facing him from across the road was a timber-framed structure, maybe thirty feet in width and twenty feet in depth, with sash windows propped open in front. Atop its roof were three light poles. A tall one in the center supported a large globe. Two poles flanking it supported smaller ones. No question, they were the lights he spotted from the train.

He eased the Jeep off the road, pulling to a stop aside from a signboard that read "SOLITAIRE" in lettering that looked like it had been inscribed with a hot poker. The logical assumption was that this was the name of the place. The kind of place, he was about to discover.

As he strode to the porch, he noticed two sizable sheds to the back of the main building. Both had large, elevated rain barrels positioned against them. What looked like a fire pit rested between the two, as well as a water well. A late-model pickup truck was also parked in the back.

He hopped onto the porch and stepped to the front door. Emblazoned on it, apparently with the same hot poker used on the signboard out front, was the greeting "Knock and it shall be opened to you." He did and it was...by a man with a large sloping head to match his husky size and a receding hairline that had little room left to retreat. "Hey...come on in," he said, a somewhat surprised look on his bloated face. "We don't get many visitors here."

Adam stepped into what appeared to be at first glance a small general store, or at least the basics of one. Wooden shelves were partially filled with myriad canned goods and packaged dried fruits, along with random utensils, from pots and pans to kettles and knives. A couple of tables had clothing items stacked upon them— jeans, flannel shirts, leather belts, hats, and blankets. Positioned on the floor, next to a small service counter, were two large wooden barrels, one filled with shelled peanuts, the other with coffee beans. The floor itself was made of old hardwood and creaked to the passing of feet. Altogether, a combination food pantry and low-end neighborhood thrift store, he concluded.

"'Solitaire,' is that the name of the store or a town?" Adam asked. "If it's the latter, it must be an invisible one. I don't see much else going on."

"To tell you the truth, I don't really know," the proprietor, or whoever he was, said from behind the counter. "Around here, we just consider it a place name, for the store, the surrounding property, or the hills...take your pick. By the way, my name is Walt," he said, sticking out his hand.

"Adam," he replied, shaking it, surprised by its fleshy texture and Walt's sartorial appearance.

"What brings you out this way, Adam?" Walt asked in a gruff voice.

"The lights," he said, continuing his perusal of the shelves.

"Oh, yeah? There have been a couple of customers who've mentioned them in the past...how they spotted them from far away. Same with you?"

"Yes, from the train."

"And that's what led you here?"

"I'm the curious kind."

"Curious about what?" Walt asked back, adopting a more serious tone.

"Curious about what life is like off the beaten path."

"Well, you've found it."

He was off the beaten path, alright, Adam thought, and now it was time for him to stop beating around the bush. "Who owns this place, and why would they build it here? Surely, you don't have enough customers to keep it afloat?" he asked.

Walt chuckled. "That question is asked by nearly every new customer who comes in here, and you're right, there aren't many of them...mostly the occasional hiker or the guy testing his off-road vehicle. In wintertime, we get virtually nobody. As for the owner, all I know is it's run by a foundation."

"Foundation?" Adam asked incredulously. "For a charitable purpose?"

"You got me. I just work here. Answered an ad in the paper and was offered the job."

"By whom?" Adam asked, puzzled by the guy's lack of curiosity as to the purpose behind the foundation.

"By a bank in Reno that acts as the agent for the outfit."

"Has the foundation got a name?"

"It's called the Hastings Foundation."

"Is it located in Reno?"

"Not sure. All I know is I drive into Reno every month to pick up my paycheck at the bank, mail at the post office, and supplies at the store to replenish whatever is needed here, which isn't much. As you can see, it's mostly dry goods we carry."

"For all practical purposes, you appear to be living off the grid, or is that how you look at it?"

"I guess you could say so, though not around the clock. Like I said, I do have to run into town on errands."

"How long have you worked here?"

"A few years. Hopefully, not much longer. I'm not a complete loner, after all, even though it's nice not having a boss looking over your shoulder all day long," he pointedly stated.

"So, how do you pass those long winter nights all alone?"

The guy reached below the counter and pulled out a deck of cards, flashing it to Adam. "Solitaire is not only the name of the place but the game of choice around here," he quipped through a plastic smile.

Adam acknowledged the lame attempt at humor with a nod, noting the seal on the deck had yet to be broken. "I see you have a shelf devoted to old books," he said.

Walt glanced at the shelf in question, as if he had forgotten it was there. "Oh, right, sometimes the hikers like to carry reading material along with them. Don't ask me why...I never was able to read and walk at the same time," he said, in another painful stab at humor.

Adam took a moment to browse the titles, taking a seat on one of two folding chairs placed against a small table that served as a reading area. None of the works did he recognize, most having to do with hiking and associated topics. Whereupon, he rose from his chair and stepped away from the shelves to glance out one of the back windows.

"How's the view from your backyard?" he asked, approaching the line between being generally interested and nosy.

Walt shrugged. "I tell you what...why don't I give you a quick tour. It's not like I don't have a lot of time on my hands."

Adam followed him out a rear door to a large flattened area upon which stood the two sheds he saw upon his arrival. Situated between them was the fire pit and water well. "That shed to your left serves as a storage bin. The shed on the right is a combination of outhouse and shower. The rain barrels positioned next to the sheds are used to catch the runoff from the roofs."

"You have running water?"

"No, we don't. The shower is the old bucket of water above your head type with the pull-down rope. We can draw water from both the well and the rain barrels. There's also a creek about a mile further up the road where you can bathe during the summer months. Otherwise, we have to heat up some water on the fire pit or on the wood stove inside."

"Do you ever get snowed in?"

"Occasionally, but it's usually not a lengthy one—maybe a week or so at the most."

"Why the rain barrels when you have a well?"

"The barrels came first. We keep them as an insurance policy. Wells can run dry, you know."

"So, while here, you are completely off the grid."

"Yes and no. We do have an electric generator inside or else we wouldn't be able to keep those lights atop the building on."

"Why have those lights? It's not like you have any significant after-hours business...or am I missing something?"

"The foundation requires it. Why, I don't know. Like I said, all I do is work here and collect a paycheck."

"And live here, I take it. I can't imagine having to make the commute every day unless there's a simpler way up here."

"Did you see the stairwell inside?"

"I did."

"It leads to an upstairs loft that serves as a bedroom."

Walt slapped his hands together. "Well, anything you'd like to take with you...bag of peanuts...some dried fruit...bottled water?" he asked, hinting for an end to the conversation.

"Make it two bags of peanuts," Adam said, feeling he shouldn't leave empty-handed.

His host stuffed two bags of the nuts to the brim and offered them to Adam for a buck each. He then bid him farewell. "Maybe we'll see you again one day," he said.

"I do have one final question, if you don't mind," Adam said, knowing full well he might be setting off alarm bells. Snatching his billfold from his back pocket, he plucked from it a photo of Jeb Lanigan that Cal had furnished him and held it up to Walt. "Ever see this guy around these parts?"

Walt quickly shook his head no, perhaps a little too quickly. "Is he wanted by the law?" he joshed.

"No, he's wanted by me," Adam said with a slight smile, before grabbing his peanuts and heading for the door.

———

ADAM SAT in his Jeep and contemplated the conversation he just had with Walt and the red flags that kept popping up. First of all, the guy and the locale were not a match. A rugged, rural lifestyle does not leave you with soft hands and a sallow complexion. Nor was the outfit he had on—silk shirt and pants, along with suede shoes—recommended clothing for the great outdoors. He could understand the startled look on the guy's face when he first entered the store. After all, the walk-in traffic, as he explained, was either light or non-existent, depending on the season. The look in his eyes, as brief as it was when he flashed him the photo of Jeb Lanigan, revealed a similar surprise. Sometimes you just don't have time to conceal your feelings when the totally unexpected hits you in the face, particularly if it's threatening. In addition, who was the "we" he kept referring to, or was it simply a subconscious reference to the mysterious foundation behind the operation? Finally, where was the garden? A garden was at the top of most off-the-grid lists, from what he understood. Perhaps the quality of the soil did not allow it. Still, there was always the boxed beds option, something his wife took to with zeal when building her vegetable garden. As for the water, there was a plentiful supply of that what with the rain barrels and the well. Plus, the stream was only a mile away, according to Walt.

So, let's make that my next stop, he decided.

Adam lowered the Jeep's windows to soak in the fresh mountain air, ignited the engine, and continued on the bumpy road inland. His path took him past a vast array of trees and shrubs, supported by a floor of fractured granite rock and turf. He glanced at his mileage gauge, showing that he had traveled more than a mile from Solitaire and yet no sign of a stream to be seen. So much for Walt's water source, he thought, when lo and behold, he rounded a bend and the creek came into view, snaking through a forest of pine trees from the slopes above.

He slowed the Jeep to a stop where the path intersected with the creek. He estimated the depth of the swift-flowing water to be no more than two feet on average. He could easily ford it and continue on but opted instead to park the vehicle on a graveled section of the bank to reflect on what got him to this point. Once settled into the scene, the first thing that came to mind was the unlikelihood of Walt gathering buckets of water and piling them into his pickup to haul them back to Solitaire. He was not the Paul Bunyan type, to say the least. So, what did all of this have to do with Jeb Lanigan's disappearance? Plenty, he reckoned, if what his intuition was telling him was true—that Jeb had set foot on Solitaire property, including the store. His mind kept going back to the instant he flashed the photo to Walt. In the course of his career, he had witnessed the reactions of a countless number of individuals having a photo suddenly shoved in front of them for purposes of identification. For Adam, it is in that first instant the eye of the beholder lets slip the liar lurking within him.

Adam hopped from the Jeep and brushed from his long-sleeved t-shirt and cargo pants crumbs from a can of trail mix he had finished off. He looked down at his sneakers and decided they still had plenty of life left in them, so he embarked on a trek up the slope, following the path of the creek. Along the way, he kept an eye out for any sign of human activity—a cabin in the woods, tents, backpackers, hunters, bikers, archeologists, as well as any wanderers, like himself, unsure of their direction. In time, he came upon a small waterfall. A large flat rock lay aside it, an open invitation for him to rest his feet. But first, he wanted to fulfill a lifelong dream and dip them in a clear mountain stream. Hurriedly, he shed his shoes and socks and lowered his limbs into the cool current. Leaning back on his elbows, he surveyed the immense scene from the High Sierra to the valley below, while listening to the burbling of the creek and surrounding birdsong. *Everywhere you look, splendor surrounds you,* he observed from his vantage point. The closest experience he could compare this to back home was when he stretched out on a lawn chair in his spacious backyard to take an afternoon nap, just about the time a neighbor would fire up his leaf blower.

He ended his oneness with nature and headed back to his Jeep. Halfway there, he became aware that he was no longer alone. From the corner of his eye, he caught a movement emanating from the deep shadows of the woods closely bordering the stream. An animal, and not the human kind, he discerned from its shape. He continued on, and so did the animal. Undoubtedly, it was trailing him, more out of curiosity than predatory instincts, he sensed.

Reaching the Jeep, Adam opened the door and grabbed from the front seat a banana he had brought along. He then leaned against the front fender, pealed it, and facing the woods, started to nibble on the fruit. Slowly, the shadow moved forward and emerged completely out of the dark into the bright sunlight. A black lab, he noted, and none the worse for wear, though understandably skittish. He broke off a piece of the banana and tossed it several feet toward the canine.

"There you go, buddy," he said, as an invitation to join him. The lab cocked his head, wagged his tail a few times, and with no further hesitation pounced on the treat. He wore no collar, leading Adam to believe he was driven up here and abandoned by some jerk. He quickly returned to the Jeep, retrieved the empty can of trail mix and a cannister of bottled water. Pouring the latter into the former, he laid it in front of the canine who commenced to lap it up.

"You got a name?" he asked the preoccupied stray. "Well, you do now. Since I first saw you hiding in the shade, I hereby christen you Shady, though I don't consider you as shady as Walt, that guy I was talking to earlier."

"Is that your dog?" a voice called out from behind him.

Adam turned to see two strapping young backpackers approaching.

"He is now, or at least for the time being," he answered.

One of the two fellows stooped to pet the dog who welcomed the attention with tail-wagging delight. "Has he got a name?"

"Shady."

"Man, I bet he's a chick magnet," the other fellow volunteered.

Adam held up his ring finger.

"Unless, of course, you're married," the guy said, quickly backtracking.

"How often do you fellows hike these hills?" he asked.

"First time for us," the chick-magnet guy said.

Adam pulled from his pocket the photo of Jeb Lanigan and flashed it to them. "Did you happen to come across this guy in your travels?"

Both took a gander at the picture. Both nodded no.

"Did you notice any camps or cabins along the way?"

"There is a rock cabin about ten miles back down this path we're on," the fellow petting Shady responded. "It's visible from the trail but appears abandoned."

The two bid him farewell and continued on their way. For an instant, it looked as if Shady debated going with them. However, the banana apparently settled the matter, as he remained on his haunches, inquisitively looking up at him in anticipation of his next move.

Adam opened the passenger side door. "Get in," he said to the stray, who obliged him immediately.

They crossed the creek and headed farther along the narrow path. The trail gradually took them higher and deeper into the woods, out from under the unimpeded glare of the midday sun. Instead, streams of sunlight filtered through the canopy of tall pines, providing an ethereal glow to the passing landscape. Meanwhile, Shady was sniffing the contents of the brown bag containing the snacks Adam had brought along. With a free hand, he grabbed one of the protein bars, opened it with his teeth, and tossed it to the dog, who wasted no time devouring it.

Nearing ten miles distance from the creek, Adam slowed the Jeep from its already deliberate pace to a crawl, eyeing the surrounding area for the cabin the hikers had mentioned. Sure enough, it was clearly visible, made more so by a shaft of sunlight streaming down through the tall pines onto the clearing on which it stood, not more than fifty yards from the trail.

Adam eased the Jeep down a footpath leading to the cabin, steering it through trees with enough separation to allow him passage. Once aside the abode, he parked on a gravel portion of the grounds and hopped from the vehicle with Shady close on his heels. Circling the tiny cabin, he noted it was made of carved stone with a wooden roof overlaid by thick moss. Windows on each side of the structure were shuttered. The entranceway was simply a series of stepping stones leading to a wooden front door. "Anybody home?" he called out, knocking on the door. There was no answer. He tried the door knob, but it was locked. He took several steps back to give the cabin a final look.

Interesting structure and locale, he ruminated. *But was it relevant to his mission? Possibly so*, he concluded.

On leaving, he passed what looked to be a burn barrel off to the side of the property. He stopped to take a closer look, lifting the lid of the incinerator to view the inside. It was empty.

"Shady!" he called out on heading back to the Jeep, having lost track of his companion. A moment later, the lab burst from behind a thicket of trees, flushed with energy from his romp into the woods. It was then Adam spotted another item of interest. Strung over one of the higher pine tree limbs was a pair of boots, fastened together by their laces. He had heard of this so-called tradition before and the myriad reasons for it, including the notion it was a way for rural folk to mark their territory or travelers to proclaim "I was once here." Nevertheless, it remained a mystery to him why a person would remove his or her shoes, tie them together, and toss them high over a tree limb for everyone to see in an area where there were few people to view them in the first place.

Looking for any kind of a lead, Adam shinnied up the tree and retrieved the boots from the limb, immediately sending Shady into a sniffing frenzy upon his descent. "Easy, buddy, we'll examine these later," he said, as they headed back to the Jeep. Reaching it, Adam tossed the boots into the vehicle's rear seat. "Right now, we've got to head back to town."

He was well aware the return trip would take them past Solitaire. For a time, he considered paying his old friend Walt a second visit for no better reason than to pester him for more information. However, he decided against it, believing he already had heard enough vagueness out of the guy for one day. As they approached the property, Shady, who had his head hanging out the window, suddenly let out a deep guttural growl, following it up with a rapid succession of whines and howls. "Shady...what is it?" Adam called to the dog while keeping one eye on the road. Shady ignored him, elevating his agitated state by fiercely pawing at the door. Fearing he was about to leap from the vehicle, Adam reached across the front seat to rest a firm hand on his back. "What is it, buddy?" he asked, settling him down a bit. As they neared the bend that would take them out of view, he glanced at the rearview mirror. There was Walt, standing in front of the store with his arms propped on his waist, intently watching them disappear around the curve.

CHAPTER THREE

EARLY THE FOLLOWING MORNING ADAM MADE IT HIS OPENING chore to find a collar and leash for Shady. He had caught a break, learning the hotel he was staying in was deemed "pet friendly." The front desk clerk also tipped him to the location of Jack's Outdoor Sporting Goods Store not far from the hotel. Minutes later, he was walking the aisles of the establishment with his shopping list in hand. In addition to the collar and leash, he added to his cart dog biscuits, poop bags, a compass, flashlight, throwaway camera, bear spray, protein bars galore, first aid kit, lighter, knife, bug repellent, water filter, and sleeping bag.

Back in his hotel room, he wrote his own name and office phone number on the collar. He then fit it on Shady, who displayed no objection, vigorously wagging his tail throughout the procedure.

"This looks to be old hat to you, buddy," Adam quipped, patting the pet on the head when finished. "Now, take a nap. I'll be back in a while."

His next task took him to the hotel lobby where he had noticed on his arrival a desktop computer placed to the side of the room for the benefit of guests. Plunking himself down in front of it, he launched into a search for a local historical society. Finding one called the Western Historical Research Society, he jotted down its address and phone number.

"Do you know where I can find this outfit?" he asked the desk clerk.

The young man glanced at the note handed him, pulled a street map from under the counter, and checked for its location. Once he pinpointed it, he turned the map toward Adam.

"It's right here," he said, pointing to a position on the map. "Go four blocks down this street we're on, take a right, and go two more blocks and you should see the building. It's in a newly developed, gentrified section of the downtown district."

Deciding to let Shady continue his nap rather than bringing him along, he hoofed it to the site of the historical society. It turned out to be similar in size to his detective agency back in Tampa, a comfy storefront operation located on the ground floor of a mid-sized edifice that looked to be part of a restored industrial building. Arced on its window facing the street was the moniker Western Historical Research Society, scripted in bold red lettering. Entering the office, Adam noted further evidence of the restoration effort. Bare, red brick walls, no doubt originating from the earlier structure, dominated the look of the single room. A wooden floor and wooden shelves replete with books were on display, along with carefully spaced potted plants. Across the ceiling ran two rows of muted track lighting. Positioned toward the back of the room was a workstation with a desktop computer. An upholstered executive chair was situated behind it. Occupying the chair was a middle-aged man wearing a brown tweed sport coat with elbow patches and a high-collared pink shirt. He had a tanned, tight face framed by thick graying hair brushed stylishly to the nape of his neck. The semblance of a smile formed on his lips as Adam approached.

"What can I do for you?" he asked, shifting his gaze from the computer to the visitor.

"I'm new in town, looking for any information on a place called Solitaire located in the Sierra foothills, a relatively short distance from Verdi."

The man behind the desk extended his hand. "George Riley," he said, introducing himself with vigor.

"Adam Fraley," his visitor said, shaking the firm hand.

"Have you tried the chamber of commerce?" Riley asked in a perfunctory manner.

"Should I?"

"No, you came to the right place." Riley motioned to one of two upholstered guest chairs fronting his desk. "Have a seat, and tell me how you came to know of Solitaire."

"I'm a wanderer by nature," Adam said, sliding his slender frame into one of the cushy chairs. "On one of my treks through the hills, I came across it. I'm not sure if it's the name of a community or what. There's a functioning general store there, and that's about it. Being the curious guy I am, I'm interested in learning how and why it came to exist in such a remote spot and what purpose it serves. In other words, what keeps the place afloat?"

Riley pushed his chair back a bit from the desk, crossed his legs, and clasped his hands in his lap, his nearly invisible smile still fixed on his face, as though his visitor's curiosity piqued his own. "Did you visit the store?" he asked.

"I did."

"And did you put these questions to whoever was on duty?"

"He seemed either reluctant or uninformed as to the history of the place. 'I just work here,' was his general attitude, though he did tell me the place was funded by a foundation...the Hastings Foundation I believe he called it, which boosted my curiosity even more."

"Why would that boost your curiosity?"

"A foundation funding a general store in a remote section of the foothills? I'd say that would tweak most any passerby's curiosity."

"Any particular reason you chose to speak with me?" he asked, as though he was having second thoughts regarding Adam's choice to visit the historical society.

"You seemed the logical place to come to for local historical information."

Riley paused in response, as though debating whether to carry the conversation any further.

"Ever hear of the place or the foundation?" Adam asked, nudging him along.

"Have I ever heard of the place or the foundation," he said, repeating the question. Riley's faint smile he had been struggling to hold on to vanished completely. "Pardon me a moment," he said, as he rose from his chair and strolled to one of the shelves to retrieve a book. "Are you familiar with this title?" he asked, turning the cover face out for Adam to view... "'Emigrants Guide to Oregon and California.'"

Adam looked the tome over carefully. "Can't say I have," he said, as though somewhat versed in the subject matter.

Riley reclaimed his chair. "The author of the book is Lansford Hastings. Does that name mean anything to you?"

"Of Hastings Foundation fame?" he gibed.

"More of Hastings Cutoff fame," he replied, carefully laying the book aside.

"The Donner Party guy?" Adam responded back, recalling a mesmerizing public television documentary on the Donner Party expedition he had seen years ago.

"Yes, he's the fellow who had convinced emigrants headed for California that a shortcut through ninety miles of waterless desert was a much quicker route to their destination...mind you, this advice coming from a guy who never took the trail himself. Well, we all know how that worked out, don't we? Unlike the California Trail or the Oregon Trail, the Hastings Cutoff lacked clear markings or wagon train ruts for pioneers to follow. As a result, the expedition lost all sense of direction and spent wasted time trying to figure out exactly where they were headed from one day to the next. Consequently, they ended up in complete disarray, all due to one man's excess greed."

"I understand that by the time the wagon train eventually reached the Sierra Nevada range, a blizzard prevented the Donner Party from reaching California," Adam recollected from the documentary. "They ran out of food and resorted to cannibalism for survival."

"Yes, and not far from where we sit," Riley stated.

"Hard to believe from a present-day perspective," Adam observed. "So, how does the foundation figure into the Solitaire story?"

"As a consequence of the Donner Party tragedy, Lansford Hastings became vilified by the general public, especially so in this part of the country, as evidenced by all of the place names around here linked to the tragedy...Donner Pass...Donner Lake...Donner Memorial State Park, not to mention all of the streets from San Jose to San Francisco named after members of the party. One of the survivors even opened up a restaurant to capitalize on his story."

"Hard to imagine anyone wanting to eat at a restaurant operated by one of the survivors," Adam interjected.

"Because of the disdain shown to Lansford Hastings, his great-granddaughter, Alicia Hastings, sought to make recompense in some way for her great-grandfather's misguided ways, even if in a small, symbolic manner. In short, she was looking for a way to salve her conscience."

"Salve her conscience or restore her family's name?" Adam interjected.

"Perhaps both. Thus, she came up with the idea of building what she envisioned as a 'lighthouse in the sky' for stranded travelers. Thus, was born Solitaire."

"Have you ever traveled up that way?" Adam asked.

"Have I ever traveled up that way?" he said, resorting again to the old tactic of repeating the question to garner time to prepare a reasonable answer or an outright lie. "Some time back, a friend and I were doing a little trekking in the hills and stopped in to take a look at the place. As I learned later, the site serves less as a historical landmark than a balm for a legacy-wounded descendent who has long since passed. From what I've read and heard, she greatly enjoyed her reputation as a colorful eccentric."

Adam slipped from his shirt pocket the photo of Jeb Lanigan

and showed it to Riley. "By chance, have you ever run across this guy in your travels around town or in the hills?"

The historian gave it a quick glance. "Nope."

There's that betraying eye thing again. Two out of two...must be something in the local water...or not.

"What business are you in, Mr. Fraley?"

And why not bother to ask who the man in the photo is before hurriedly redirecting the conversation?

"Research and recovery," he answered, doing a little shading of the truth himself.

"Hmm...interesting," Riley said, before exhaling a deep breath. "Well, that's the story of Solitaire. Now, I must get to a meeting, if you'll excuse me."

———

IMMEDIATELY UPON HIS return to the hotel, Adam took Shady on a walk. Having been confined to a cramped room, the lab was overjoyed at his arrival back, launching into a spontaneous happy-feet-and-tail wagging routine that nearly toppled a desk lamp. "Easy boy," he said, as he tethered the canine to his leash. A couple of laps around the block settled the pet down. They returned to the hotel room, at which point Adam called his wife in Tampa.

"Okay, babe, I have three search requests, if you can squeeze them in today," he said.

"Fortunately, it's an unusually quiet day around here and I have a pen in hand...let's hear them."

"If I recall right, you once worked for a foundation...correct?"

"Now that's impressive, you remembering the minutia of my resume from way back when," she joshed. "Is that what got me hired?"

"Just one of the items I was dazzled with," he bantered back. "Seriously, the reason I ask is that I need any information you can come up with on an outfit called the Hastings Foundation. It's based here in Reno."

"Got it...next?"

"Any info you can find on a place called Solitaire. It's located in the Sierra Nevada foothills near Verdi, Nevada."

"Spelled like the card game?"

"Same spelling."

"What is it exactly?"

"Good question. It could be nothing other than a patch of real estate. There's a general store located on the property, along with a signboard with that name carved on it. Whether it's the name of the store, the smallest town in the world, or the property itself, I have no idea. Also, there's what looks like a recently constructed off-the-grid stone cabin located not far from Solitaire. I have no idea of what the laws of Nevada are regarding construction in that area, but anything you can find on the subject, I'd appreciate."

"And the third item?"

"I need the phone number of Jeb Lanigan's grandmother in San Francisco. Perhaps Cal has it, or maybe not."

"Okay, I'll see what I can dig up and get back to you later on today. By the way, how are things progressing out there?"

"I'm not sure. All I have right now are a couple of suspicions."

"Are suspicions equivalent to leads?"

"I like to think of them as precursors, optimistic guy that I am."

———

DURING THE CONVERSATION with his wife, Adam noticed Shady had drifted asleep on the floor. Not a bad idea, he thought, considering his agenda for the day called for another excursion into the hills. How soon depended on the info his wife came up with. So, he kicked off his shoes, stretched out on the bed, and in no time joined his traveling mate in a deep slumber.

Both dog and he awoke with a start at the ear-piercing clang of the phone. He glanced at a digital clock on the nightstand. Three hours had passed since he had conversed with his wife.

In an instant, he was back on the phone with her. "I was unable to come up with much to report on," she said.

"Right now, I'll take anything you got."

"Okay, first on Solitaire...I found nothing in the public records for the area regarding it, nor anything on what could be considered a neighboring abode. However, based on my quick research, it does appear the laws of Nevada are fairly relaxed as far as off-the-grid living is concerned. Secondly, on the Hastings Foundation, I did find some basic info. Its stated mission is to provide travel assistance and travelers aid to needy individuals or organizations. It's a private, very small foundation. The traditional guideline, as I recall from my days in the business, is that you need a minimum of $250,000 of start-up money, though one to two million dollars is considered a more prudent amount. In addition, foundations are required to pay out five percent of their assets per year."

"Foundations are a good money laundering option for the underworld...right?"

"You bet, especially if it's a cash-intensive operation. For instance, money earned through a drug deal can be funneled into the banking system by pretending to the bank it came from a legitimate source—say, a flea market stall, a farmer's market stall, or a thrift store operated by a non-profit organization."

"Like cash coming from a fake general store."

"You state that as if you've run into one. You think the store you visited today is a front?"

"Maybe...How long has the Hastings Foundation been in existence?"

"Fifteen years."

"Any officers listed?"

"One...the chief officer."

"His or her name?"

"George Riley."

"My dear, you have just turned a suspicion into a lead."

"You know him?"

"He's a recent acquaintance of mine," he answered with a tinge of sarcasm.

"Adam, I took the liberty of checking a newspaper databank to see if there was further information on him. You might be interested in what showed up."

"What's that?"

"He was fired from a tenured teaching position at Valley State College in Reno."

"For what?"

"He had a gambling addiction that caused him to miss numerous classes of his, so they let him go. He fought the firing but it was upheld in a court ruling."

"How long ago was this?"

"Twenty years."

"Having been fired from a job does not prevent one from setting up a non-profit foundation, does it?"

"Believe it or not, even a felony conviction is not a bar to someone setting up a foundation in the eyes of the IRS."

"How does the IRS keep track of the legitimacy of all these non-profits?"

"Primarily through the financial records and banking activities, as well as the number and kind of complaints coming from the general public and whistleblowers."

"Don't they require a board of directors?"

"Yes, but it can be as few as three members. In many cases, they are figureheads with no real power."

"Is there a byline to the article you referenced?"

"Yes...the reporter's name is Ned Garland."

"The newspaper?"

"The Reno Beacon. Oh, and one other item regarding the Hastings Foundation. I did check their credit rating."

"Credit rating? Good or bad, how is that of benefit to us?"

"The credit rating service lists the name of their bank...Washoe State Bank."

"Good stuff...what about a phone number for Lanigan's grandmother...any luck?"

"Yes, got it right here in my notes."

Adam jotted down the number, still pumped by the Riley revelation. Better to be lucky than good, he mused.

"How is our daughter doing? Is she anxiously waiting for my return, so we can get on with her college search?"

"That and the gift for her you surely won't forget to bring back."

———

No sooner was he off the phone with his wife, than he was back on it, speaking with Lanigan's grandmother. "Who did you say you were?" she asked in a thin, breathy voice.

"Adam Fraley...I'm a private investigator, looking for your grandson."

"Jeb? I don't know where he is. I've been trying to find out his whereabouts myself. The last time I spoke with him was about five or six months ago. It's very worrisome to me because he always kept in touch up till then. Have you spoken with his friend Cal? I have and even he doesn't know."

"Yes, I spoke to him and he shares the same concern as you. Tell me, in your talks with Jeb before he disappeared, did he give any indication where he might have gone?"

She paused to collect her thoughts. "Well, I recall one thing he said that puzzled me. He said he was going off the grid, whatever that means. He tried to explain it...something about living alone in the wilds. I told him he can't grow toothbrushes or toilet paper in the wild. I asked him to explain the reason for his decision, but all he would say is that it was something he always wanted to do."

"Anything else you can recall?"

"Yes, he said he was building a stone cabin to live in. He had finished the exterior and was about to start on the interior."

"But he didn't say where?"

"No, though when I asked where he was getting his groceries, he sort of laughed and said, for the time being, he was getting them at a nearby store."

"Nearby store?"

"Yes...one that was a short driving distance from his cabin. And here I was thinking living off the grid meant living in the wilds and being self-sufficient, but I guess not. Oh, and I asked him how Shadow was doing. He said fine."

"Shadow?"

"Yes...his dog. Is he missing too?"

Adam glanced at his canine sidekick, who had reared up on his hind legs at the mention of his name. "No, he's no longer missing."

"Good gracious, I don't know what to make of that. Jeb would never go off and leave Shadow. They were like two peas in a pod."

"Hopefully, they won't be separated for much longer," he said, consoling the woman. "We'll let you know when we find out anything."

"Please do."

Done with the phone calls, Adam walked over to where the lab rested on his haunches, bending down to place his hands firmly on each side of his head, drawing it close to his grinning face. He vigorously stroked the dog behind its ears. "So...Shadow it is," he said, the pet licking his face in return as if saying, "I like you, too." Adam then uttered the words dear to every lab's heart. "Now, let's go hunting."

CHAPTER FOUR

Adam stuffed a backpack he had brought along from Tampa with the supplies he had purchased earlier in the day, including a pen from his hotel room and night goggles, another item he had carted from home. Surveillance was the bread and butter of his business, and that was an around-the-clock chore. Admittedly, they were behind in applying the latest technology to their craft, something his wife continually reminded him about whenever the matter of cellphone usage arose. "Yes, it's the first thing on the agenda when I return," he would assure her.

By twilight, they had reached Solitaire. Adam eased by the store, noting there were no vehicles in sight. He continued on crossing the creek on the path to the stone cabin he had visited. He decided a second look was in order since they had little else in the form of clues to pursue at this stage.

With Shadow by his side, he circled the cabin once again on foot. All appeared unchanged. He tugged at the front door with the same result as before. On a whim, he scanned the grounds around the entrance for places to stash away a backup key. All for nothing, it turned out...no mats...no rocks...no flower pots to serve as hideaways.

Shadow, meanwhile, was leaping and pawing at the door. "Easy boy," he said. "You look a lot like me trying to climb that tree over there yesterday."

Adam's eyes shifted to the tree he was referencing.

Could it be?

"Sit tight here, Shadow," he commanded, pointing to the ground. "I'll be back in a minute."

Adam jogged over to the Jeep to retrieve the boots he had stashed in the back seat. He took the first in hand and checked the interior, finding nothing out of the ordinary. In checking the second, he did find something askew...a key that was taped to the insole. He removed it and hustled back to the cabin's front entrance where Shadow waited impatiently. He hurriedly slipped the key into the lock and, to his delight, it was a match. He swung the door open and entered, the lab close on his heels.

The abode's dimly lit interior appeared unlived in, with but a few pieces of furniture, including an army cot, scattered over a stone slab floor. A cast-iron stove and vent stood positioned in one corner, also appearing unused. No items of a personal nature were to be seen. It was as though the move-in had hardly begun before it was interrupted...or ended. Shadow, especially, seemed disappointed by the emptiness of it all, halting his energized sniffing around and tail wagging to settle on all fours, like a spinning top having wound down.

Adam reached out and tapped the lab's head. "Keep your chin up, my friend. The hunt has just begun."

———

ADAM LOCKED the door of the cabin and returned to the patch of land where he had parked the Jeep the previous day. He sat aside the Jeep, amid the shadowy pines, munching on a protein bar, at the same time feeding his traveling companion several of the dog biscuits. Darkness had descended over the foothills, bringing to life the nocturnal chorus of insects, accompanied by the steady gurgling of the nearby creek. Occasionally, the solitary cry of a distant animal and the flutter of wings from an unseen source, punctuated the rhythmic sounds, adding an element of mystery to the night.

"You know, Shadow, I once had a dog back in my bachelor days. It was an Ibizan hound...purebred. Bought him from a guy in Missouri. Drove all the way up from Florida to get him. I named him Shu, after an Egyptian god in honor of his heritage. Shu was the god of light and air—much like the atmosphere you see around us now. He was a handsome dog, alright...that's not to say he was handsomer than you," he quickly added, tossing the lab another biscuit.

"One day I let him out in the backyard to play. In those days, leash laws were not what they are today. You could pretty much let pets like you roam as they please, as long as you kept them in sight. Besides, my backyard was fenced in—a six-foot-high barrier —high enough to keep Shu from leaping over it, according to a pet-loving friend of mine who considered himself an expert on the subject." Adam took another bite out of the protein bar. "Well, Shadow, I should have sought out an expert on the breed. One evening I went out back to feed him and he was gone. I later learned it's possible for an Ibizan to clear a six-foot-high fence from a standing position, something you might even be able to do. Anyway, I went looking for him in my pickup, scouring the streets for a sign of him. At one point, my search was interrupted when I came upon a young woman standing beside her car in the middle of a street. She was sobbing into her hands. I decided to stop and see what was causing her distress, thinking her car may have broken down. She told me a deer had darted out in front of her and she had hit it. At first glance, I saw no deer. 'Did it take off?' I asked her, figuring the deer had survived the blow. She shook her head, her face still buried in her hands. 'He's under the car,' she mumbled through her sobs. I then took one look under the vehicle. 'Lady, that's no deer,' I said to her. 'That's my dog,' which immediately launched her into another crying spell. There was nothing I could do for Shu. He was dead. It was understandable. An Ibizan has large erect ears and a tawny coat. Throw in the dimness of the evening and it could easily be mistaken for a small deer."

Adam reached out and patted his companion on the head. Shadow had his snout on the ground and expressive eyes looking up at him as if trying to understand the meaning of the tale. "The lesson I learned, Shadow, was a simple one. I was not cut out to be a pet owner...end of story."

The two lapsed into a silence, allowing the gentle rustling of leaves to lull them into a lethargic state...that was until a shrill cacophony of blood-curdling squeals arising from the bowels of the forest pierced the nighttime air. Instantly, Shadow was on his feet and racing toward the ruckus.

"Shadow...hold on!" Adam called out, as he reached into the Jeep to grab his backpack before hustling to catch up with the lab. Entering the thick of the woods, he held out a hand to ward off unseen limbs while side-stepping clumps of bushes as best he could in the dark. With his free hand, he reached into his bag and donned his night goggles, which revealed a pale-green image of what lay in his path. The squeals morphed into a series of grunts and snarls the closer he approached the source...evidence that Shadow, running twenty yards out in front of him, had joined the commotion that was centered in a small clearing ahead. The scene quickly unfolded the moment he reached it. Three feral boars, their snouts in the ground, were foraging for food. They had dug from the ground what looked like a large burlap sack. They already had ripped it apart and were working on removing the innards. Shadow, however, was hindering their efforts by annoying the hell out of them with his barking and fake attacks on their position. One of the boars broke from the pack and took after the lab, but Shadow was much too quick for it, and easily escaped the animal's razor-sharp tusks. Realizing the futility of taking on the lab, the hog rejoined his mates.

Having ripped open the burlap sack, the boars next took on the exposed contents. From where he stood in the shadows, Adam made them out to be extra-large zippered storage bags, containing some sort of powdered substance. In an instant, the hogs sliced into one of them, burying their noses in the powder and sniffing it thoroughly. It became obvious the stuff did not appeal to their appetites, as they immediately lost interest in their discovery and wandered off back into the woods, Shadow giving them several going-away growls for good measure.

Adam stepped out from the shadows to inspect the area, in particular the bag that had been ripped open. He took a knee and dipped a finger into the white powder and tapped his tongue to taste it. Cocaine, as he expected. "Keep your nose out of it," he snapped at Shadow who had his own snout buried in the stuff. For a moment, he debated whether to take one of the bags as evidence the underground burial site existed. In the end, he decided against it, figuring the risk of getting caught with it on his person, outweighed the greater good of his mission. Instead, he plucked the camera from his backpack and took several shots of the stuff, before continuing his inspection. The one other foreign item he spotted was a castaway cellophane wrapper containing a half-eaten stick of licorice. He picked it up, noted the Devil's Tail brand, and stuffed it into his back pocket.

Finished with his inspection, he took a step back to size up the situation. For sure, it was the work of drug traffickers. Unfortunately for them, the hogs had exposed their stash and perhaps something more important...a possible connection to his mission. They stood approximately a half-mile from the creek. Off in the distance, in the opposite direction, stood Solitaire, its towering lights visible through the treetops.

"Let's head back to the creek, Shadow. We'll crash there for the night. First thing in the morning, we'll make a visit to Solitaire to stir the pot."

CHAPTER FIVE

The reaction of the Solitaire store clerk to Adam's morning appearance was not unlike that of a newlywed on seeing his in-laws from hell showing up unexpectedly on his doorstep on his wedding night.

Walt nodded his hello, as he entered the store. Adam at once noticed a man sitting atop the closed lid of the wooden barrel containing the peanuts.

"Good morning," Adam said in a civil tone, at once commencing his browsing of the shelves.

"Found that buddy of yours yet?" Walt asked.

"No...but I wanted to ask if you know anything about that stone cabin ten or so miles past the creek."

"Not much. I was told it belonged to one of those living-off-the-grid guys who sometimes show up in the hills. The truth is, I really don't pay much attention to people looking to live off the grid. They come up here with their pockets full of money and their pickups stacked with supplies, believing they can make a go of it. No, we're more interested in helping those lost adventurers who are attempting to find the grid."

"Oh, yes, your mission...to aid stranded travelers in memory of the Donner party."

Walt continued his sudden harangue, ignoring the mission statement he had probably never heard recited before. "The off-the-grid wannabes who come up here and don't have the faintest idea of what life is like in these parts soon learn they are in way over their head. Maybe your friend came to realize that and went back to where he belonged."

"Did I say he was a guy looking to live off the grid?"

"Are you telling me he wasn't?" came the testy reply.

"How many wayward travelers would you say you've encountered over the years?"

"Including you?"

"Sure...including me, since you may have set me on the right path."

"We don't keep a running tally," he muttered.

Walt was not having a good start to the day, Adam reckoned. "The best liars lead off spouting truths to establish believability," his old boss once advised him long ago. "Once that's accomplished, they can follow with their damned lies." This guy either didn't buy into that approach or simply didn't have the patience for it. For whatever reason...perhaps because of his sarcastic reference to Solitaire's mission...his disposition had undergone a dramatic transformation from the previous day. He had come to stir the pot, but Walt already appeared stoked. Mission accomplished.

Throughout his exchange with Walt, the man who no doubt owned the all-terrain vehicle that Adam noticed parked outside on his way in was paying close attention to the give-and-take. He was casually sitting atop the closed peanut barrel with his legs crossed, puffing on a slim stogie, its smoke rings curling upward past a vintage Non-Smoking sign nailed to the wall. The guy was doing a good impression of movie bad guy Jack Palance, Adam observed. He had dark, beady eyes brimming with evil intent and a sharp, taut face upon which was chiseled a thin sardonic smile that silently shouted, "I'm going to savor every bit of misery I'm about to inflict on you." He was dressed in jeans, a tanned shirt, a wide-brimmed canvas hat, and worn boots. He also had a fixed blade knife strapped to his side. Obviously, the guy wasn't there to welcome customers, Adam quipped to himself.

"You looking for supplies?" Walt asked, as Adam casually browsed the shelves, "or are you still in search of your lost pal? If so, you're piling up a lot of wasted time that could be put to better use elsewhere." In other words, get the hell out of here.

"Just looking for the truth," Adam responded. "What is it they say...truth is a moving target...could be anywhere...say, even on these shelves."

"Well, that makes the truth seeker an even bigger target...don't you think?" Walt countered in a menacing tone.

"Maybe so. By the way, do you have video cameras mounted outside?" Adam asked, continuing with his poking.

"Why should we? And tell me...are you a cop?"

"I'm the guy you referenced a moment ago...a truth seeker. It seems reasonable to me my friend would have stopped by here at least occasionally for supplies."

Walt was becoming less amiable with every passing exchange, which suited Adam fine. He should have stuck with the persona he adopted the moment they first met...the friendly country rube. Once that was firmly established, he could have easily followed with his lies.

Adam pulled a can of peaches from a shelf and held it up for Walt to see. "Expiration date has passed," he said, drawing a glare from the proprietor.

"You got an expiration date?" the guy atop the peanut barrel asked.

"Not that I'm aware of," Adam responded. "How about you? Do you know your expiration date?"

"No, I don't know mine, but I do know yours."

A slight smile creased Adam's face. "By the way, did either of you hear all that commotion coming from the woods last night?" he asked. "Sounded like an animals' night out."

Walt exchanged a quick glance with Mr. Mean Looking. "What is it...you got a base camp set up around here to monitor all of the local activities?"

Adam ignored the comment. "Okay, I've decided what I need," he said, stepping away from the shelves.

"What's that?" Walt said, seemingly relieved that the end of the visit was near.

"A large sack of peanuts."

Certainly, that's not the way Walt wanted it to end, Adam reckoned. He was hoping for a fast, civil departure.

Walt gave a quick glance to his cohort planted on the barrel before reaching under the counter for an empty sack. Adam took it and strode toward the barrel. Mr. Mean Looking gave no indication he was about to abandon his perch, much less the nasty demeanor.

Adam politely gestured for him to move aside, so he could fill his peanut sack. Instead, the guy stuck with his manner, relishing the palpable tension he was generating in the room.

"Cruel, get the hell up," Walt commanded from across the room.

Adam chuckled to himself. *So, Cruel is the name,* he mused. *How appropriate. I can imagine the fun his confederates and enemies must have bestowing nicknames on him. Come to think of it, that could well be the moniker given him.*

Cruel slithered off the barrel in a painstakingly slow manner and stood to the side, allowing Adam to fill his sack. "Oh, and one another item I could use," he said, addressing his request to Walt. "Do you, by chance, have any licorice?"

Walt reached to grab an item out of a carton behind the counter and handed it to Adam, hoping no doubt this was the last of the visitor's requests. "Is that it?" he snorted.

"That's it," he replied, reaching for his billfold to pay for the items. As he turned to leave, he caught one last glimpse of Cruel, back on his perch, the intensity in his eyes having been hiked a notch or two.

Adam's own curiosity intensified when he noticed the logo on the licorice wrapping—it was the Devil's Tail brand.

———

ADAM SAT in the Jeep out front of the store pondering his next move, all the while giving Shadow a backrub. In the midst of it, a dark brown van crawled into view from the creek side of Solitaire. It marked the first time he had seen another vehicle while traversing the trail.

The van eased onto the store property, paying him no heed. Two day-laborer types, husky and full of chatter, hopped from the vehicle and strode into the store. Their visit could be innocent enough, he figured, though the direction from which they came, suggested another possibility.

"Time to retrace our steps," he said to Shadow, ending the backrub. He jotted down the license plate number of the van, ignited his rental, and steered it back onto the trail. He headed along the path to the creek, pulling the vehicle to a stop at a point along the way that, in his estimation, was close to the site of the buried cocaine cache they had stumbled upon the previous night.

He attached the leash to Shadow's collar. "Don't want you to go chasing after feral pigs, buddy." The dog immediately stretched the leash to its length, undoubtedly sensing their destination point.

In nothing flat, they were standing aside the site. It had undergone a complete makeover. The holes had been plugged, the turf raked level, and brush scattered over it. Sure, there was a chance the cache was reburied, but not likely, Adam concluded, given the risk of the hogs returning for a second look. More than likely, it was carted away, conceivably by the two men in the van that showed up at the store.

Adam realized he now had a choice to make...pursue the drug trafficking operation or stick to his primary mission of tracking down Jeb Lanigan. Sure, there was a likelihood the two were linked, he admitted, but this was no time to get sidetracked. Not only did he have no police powers, there was no way to contact them at the moment without returning to town. He certainly wasn't going to revisit the store to see if a phone was available. He already knew the answer to that. Nope, the choice was clear.

"Time to climb those hills, Shadow," he said, sending the lab into another tail-wagging frenzy.

CHAPTER SIX

A weak cool front had pushed its way through the hills, turning an otherwise warm summer day into a hiker's delight. Adam quickly reminded himself that it was not a hike they were embarking on, but a mission with an ending far less certain in its trajectory.

He parked the Jeep behind the abandoned stone cabin which would serve as the trailhead, though the trail they were taking would be of their own design, determined in most part by Shadow's nose. In keeping with the latter intent, he snatched from the back seat the boots he had retrieved from the tree and passed them again under the lab's snout. He had read somewhere that a scent on the ground is viable for anywhere up to 14 days or more.

Adam strapped on his backpack and tethered Shadow to the leash. Moments later, they were crossing the trail they came in on and headed up the hillside. It was an inauspicious beginning, however, when Adam inadvertently stepped on a beehive. The ensuing commotion sent Shadow and him scrambling in every direction to escape the wrath of the bees. Eventually, they did, emerging without a sting, and soon were back to climbing the hillside, circumventing tall shrubs while trying not to trip over tree roots or bang into low-hanging limbs. For Adam, it was tantamount to an obstacle course, for Shadow it was a walk in the park.

The pattern of the topography they were negotiating soon became apparent. They were climbing a series of gradual rises marked by stands of trees, each rise followed by a similarly small meadow featuring boulders of varying sizes and shapes lying amid carpets of wildflowers.

After the initial encounter with the bees, the ascent went smoothly. Adam's familiarity with the lay of the land gradually grew, as did his confidence in traversing it. That was, until the ground literally fell out from under him.

———

HE LOOKED SKYWARD, through the narrow tunnel leading to the opening of the cave into which he had fallen. Shadow was circling the opening, barking steadily at the man at the bottom. Adam interpreted it in canine speech as, "You idiot...watch where you're going." His instinct was to bark back, "I was watching where I was going. And why didn't you warn me?"

In truth, he had fallen victim to one of Mother Nature's uncommon occurrences. The small cave's opening was camouflaged by layers of brush and leaves accumulated over time. He was lucky Shadow was traveling off to his side when it happened or else both of them would have disappeared into the nether world. As it was, he had enough sense to let loose of the leash to keep it from happening. Lucky too that he had landed on his feet, his fall slowed by sprouts of underground tree limbs and cushioned at the bottom by a large pile of dead leaves and twigs, the latter emitting a strong earthly odor.

Adam took measure of his predicament. Whether it was a cave, a cavity, a sinkhole, or simply a hole in the ground was a moot point. His job now was not to define but to escape. He slipped off his backpack and retrieved his flashlight, running its beam first over his body to gauge the seriousness of the scrapes and bruises he had received. None rose to a serious level, he concluded. Nor were there broken bones, as far as he could tell. He next turned the beam on the floor around him, relieved to find no creepy-crawly creatures or skeletal bones. Continuing with his assessment, he estimated the width of the hole at four feet, narrow enough for him to extend his arms and place the palms of his hands against both sides of the cave's cylindrical walls, composed of a mix of packed mud and rock. Anything more confining and his claustrophobia would have kicked in by now.

"Shadow...Shadow! Quiet down up there!" he called up to the lab, concerned the dog's steady barking might draw the attention of unwelcome predators. True to his command, the barking ceased, replaced by an occasional whimper.

He returned his attention to the dimensions of his underground prison, specifically the depth of the cavity, which he estimated at approximately twenty feet. He figured a skilled climber could probably scale the wall as is, utilizing the existing cracks and protruding rock as props. However, he was nowhere near that skill level.

He recalled the last time he faced a vertical climb of similar dimensions. It came during an Air Force basic training obstacle course exercise that called for him to scale a 25-foot wall with the aid of a rope attached to the top of the barrier. Also fastened to the rim of the wall was a bell with a pull rope. Upon completion of the climb, recruits were instructed to ring the bell to signal they had completed the exercise. The wall climb was the final obstacle on the outdoor course, which added to the difficulty of it since most recruits were exhausted by this stage. When his turn came, it was not so much his lack of energy as it was his sweaty hands that led to an embarrassing moment. As he neared the top of the wall, the rope slipped from his grasp. His immediate instinct was to grab the closest thing in sight for support, which was the bell rope. For the next half-minute, he swung back and forth from it with one hand, like a monkey on a tree limb. If that wasn't embarrassing enough, the incessant clanging of the bell drew the full attention of onlookers, including his drill sergeant. "Hey, Fraley!" he bellowed out. "Stop with the showboating and get your ass over the wall!"

One final swing enabled him to reach out and regain his grip on the wall rope. Thus, was he able to complete the climb without further drama.

"Maybe you should get back to the task at hand," he muttered under his breath, ending his recollection.

He scrutinized the situation one last time. If he was to make it to the top, he would need to carve out a vertical succession of footholds and handholds at intervals of two to three feet, he estimated.

He rummaged through the backpack for his knife. Once in hand, he slipped the pack back on and commenced with the building of the earthen ladder. He carved out the first four holds from a standing position, making sure they were of sufficient size to accommodate his hands and feet. Another freefall and he might not be as fortunate in avoiding protruding rocks and serious injury.

He wedged his feet into the bottom holds. From there he reached up past the second holds to carve out another set of holds. He would repeat the process until his ladder reached the top of the wall.

His climb was not without incident. Halfway up, the knife nearly slipped from his grip when he struck it hard against a mud-covered rock. Losing the knife would have slowed the process immeasurably, leaving him with the decision of whether to retreat back down to recover it or proceed on, utilizing his fingers to claw out the remaining holds.

He was five feet from the top, when a strange occurrence disrupted his concentration, halting his advance. From above ground came a fierce exchange of guttural snarls, followed by a cascade of brush and dirt rushing into the cave, clouding the air. Adam instinctively closed his eyes and held his breath to avoid inhaling the grit. The commotion died out as quickly as it arose.

"Shadow! What the hell's going on up there? Are those boars back?" he shouted out, hurriedly resuming his climb. He carved out the final two holds and pocketed his knife. At that point, he stretched a free hand onto the surface bordering the opening. Finding a firm piece of turf to grip, he placed a second hand beside it, and in one fell swoop, used his arms and legs to launch himself onto the surface. Back on solid ground, he rolled over on his back, drew in a deep breath and exhaled it. He glanced over at Shadow who was resting on all fours, a look of innocence tacked onto his face, as though nothing out of the ordinary had happened during his absence.

"What was the ruckus all about?" he asked, drawing a side-eye look from the lounging lab. "For a minute there, I thought someone was trying to bury me alive." He surveyed the area. "Never mind," he said, spotting from the corner of his eye a young coyote disappearing into the woods across the way. "I've found the answer to my question." He leaned over to whisper to the lab, "Now I have another one, did you get the best of him?"

"Woof!"

Adam fished from his backpack a bottle of water. Nearby was a large stone with a concave surface. He poured half of the bottle into it for Shadow. "Drink up," he said, before guzzling down the other half. "We've lost valuable time. Got to get back on the trail."

———

THE HILLS WERE BECOMING STEEPER, slowing their pace. At one point, they were confronted by a large stretch of stacked deadwood, requiring some nimble footwork on the part of both of them to traverse it. Adam checked his compass. They were traveling in a west-northwest direction. According to his calculation, it meant they were likely headed for a rendezvous with the creek sometime soon. Where all this was leading to, he had no idea. He was pinning his hopes on Shadow. Thus far, the lab was giving indications he did know, as evidenced by his demonstrably higher energy level and all-out effort to keep his nose to the ground.

In time, the creek came into view through the spaced trees. Not only could they see it, but they also could hear it, due to the presence of the gurgling waterfall he had come upon on his first trek up the hillside.

Adam came to a stop, taking a seat on one of the many granite slabs bordering the stream. The sun was setting beyond the western peaks, leaving behind a sherbet-hued orange glow on the rim of the horizon. Shortly, nightfall would be upon them.

"We're going to spend the night here," he announced to Shadow, unhooking the dog's leash. "You and I need some rest, or at least I do. We'll give it another go first thing in the morning." What he didn't say, or admit to, was that the altitude was beginning to affect his breathing. For a guy who had spent his life mostly roaming Florida flatlands, there was no foundation to prepare him for lofty heights like these. Cleaning the gutters of his home was about as elevated as he got back home. High altitude sickness was often sudden and life-threatening, he was told by those in the know.

"Don't be foolish in weighing the risks of your job," his old boss Pete Peterson would always say. "You have a family to come home to...a responsibility that trumps all others."

He noticed the slab of rock he was sitting on had a small indentation on its surface. Removing his backpack, he retrieved a bottle of water from it, along with a handful of dog biscuits. He poured some water into the indentation and laid the biscuits aside it. "There's your dinner," he said to the lab, who wasted no time indulging himself. He, in turn, tasted a peanut from his purchase at Solitaire, which was stale. Another of the store's items that passed its expiration date, he figured. So, he commenced to devour a couple of protein bars, as well as a packet of dried fruit.

"You ever hear of the Donner Party?" he asked Shadow, between bites.

The lab continued with his own meal uninterrupted.

"You don't have a recollection of it, you say."

Shadow shifted his eyes toward him, as though realizing he was being addressed.

"They were a hearty band of pioneers with big dreams. Tried to wagon-train it all the way from Illinois to California but ended up stranded in these very hills...got stuck in snow up to twenty feet deep. Come to think of it, they could have used you as a guide to

52

help get them out." Adam paused. "Nah, on second thought, it was probably best you weren't around back then, considering how it all ended for the family dogs."

Adam removed from his backpack his sleeping bag. "I'm making my bed on top of the leaves, twigs, and bark, that make up the great mattress of the forest floor. You're welcome to join me or stay put on the slab if you choose. Should be good sleeping weather, whichever you choose."

Shadow kept his place, his snout between his front paws, his eyes following Adam's every move.

"You and that master of yours must have been best of friends...right?"

Shadow let out a muffled "woof."

"Thought so. Must be an alright guy if you like him. Means I'd like him too...don't you think?"

The lab let out a louder bark

"Hey, keep your voice down, or else you're going to wake up the dead around here. Have you already forgotten what I told you about the Donner Party? Many of them died in these hills."

"Woof."

"That's better," he said, satisfied with the response. "Before my dog died, I spent quite a bit of time reading up on human and animal interaction, particularly on how bonds are formed with pets. The authorities on the subject kept pointing to this hormone called oxytocin. Apparently, it facilitates the bonding between people and pets. Funny, how it works. According to those in the know, canines like you are loaded with the stuff. Did you know that?"

Shadow remained silent, replanting his snout on the ground and refixing his eyes on him.

"Didn't think so," Adam said, continuing on. "What produces the hormone is your constant gazing at your owner, hour after hour, and their gazing back, just like you and I are doing now. Simple as that. Takes the magic and uniqueness out of the bonding process, if you ask me. No wonder we don't know exactly when the bond takes hold. One thing we do know...people don't fall out of love with their dogs like they do with each other. There's something to think about."

"Yeah, can't wait to meet your master," Adam said, slipping into the sleeping bag.

Weary from the climb, he was soon asleep. It was a restless one, though, the unfamiliar environs working to awaken him sometime in the middle of the night. He lay there, his eyes opened to the immense sky above him, ablaze with luminous celestial bodies. Through a lattice of leaves, he spotted the moon, glowing exceptionally bright. Slowly, he traced the ethereal canvas to the earth's horizon where above the tips of the pines burned the lights of a terrestrial landmark...Solitaire. What is it the experts advise hikers when they are headed into the woods? First, find a point of reference to keep you from getting lost, since everything has a tendency to look the same. Well, from this point on Solitaire would be his guide to who knew what or where.

At last, in the wee hours of the morning, his weariness overcame his restlessness, and he drifted back to sleep.

––––––

ADAM WOKE TO A WHITEOUT. All he could see in every direction was a cascade of white flakes falling everywhere, leaving a thick blanket of pure-driven snow atop the hills and trees alike. It made for a stark black and white world, completely bereft of color, something you might see in a flickering silent film of old. Despite its starkness, he strained to bring clarity to what it was he was witnessing, as though he was viewing it through a thin veil. It appeared real, but then abruptly turned bizarre, when a horde of men, in a mass resurrection, rose from beneath the snowpack like stalks of corn. In unison, they commenced to trudge up the hillside in his direction, their deadened faces locked on his.

"Don't give up people! There's help on the way!" he yelled down to them, motioning to a nearby cluster of trees off to his side. Straight away, eight reindeer, pulling an empty giant sleigh, appeared from behind the thicket, prancing toward him. "These reindeer are going to take us over this hill to

California. I got them on loan from the Big Guy. Donner will lead the way."

"I'm Donner!" the guy leading the horde growled up to him. "I'll do the leading."

"To California? I'm telling you that you can't get to California without the help of these reindeer."

"Can't you see! Right now, we're not interested in getting to California," the leader of the pack cried out to him. "We need food! We're interested in getting to you!"

Jolted to reality, he turned to scramble up the hill, feverishly glancing behind him to see the horde gaining on him. Up ahead, the reindeer and the sleigh had gone airborne, disappearing over the crest of the hill. "Hey! Wait for me!!!" he yelled to no effect. "Yeah, you can tell Mr. Fat Guy I once believed in him!" he shouted at them. "Now, I'm not so sure!"

His chest rising and falling with rapid breaths, he paused to ponder the situation. Hell, he'd make it without them, he decided. He was a mere thirty yards from the crest of the hill. Once he reached it, he would have a clear view of the California landscape. The sight of it alone should energize him enough to complete his journey. He tried to run faster, but the drifts were growing deeper and more plentiful the higher he rose. Furthermore, his legs had turned to noodles. At last, heart racing and arms flailing, he collapsed deep into one of the snowbanks. Trapped, he lapsed into a delirious state.

Moments later, amid the clamor of the horde, he felt his face being licked. He howled to the heavens, awakening to the one doing the licking.

"Shadow!" he shrilled, sitting up to gulp down a few deep breaths. "Oh, man, I would have made a terrible pioneer," he said, collecting himself.

The lab lay by his side, inducing a calm in him and the promise of a better sleep ahead, free of nightmares.

CHAPTER SEVEN

A WOODPECKER SOUNDED THE MORNING ALARM, ITS STACCATO rat-a-tat echoing across the hillsides like distant gunfire.

"Hey, Shadow! You ready to get back to work?" Adam called to his companion who was busy pawing away at a clump of twigs and leaves a short distance away. A moment later he was trotting back, carrying in his jaws a flat foreign object of some sort.

"What do you have there?" Adam asked, taking the object from his jaws. "What the hell!" he shouted, bursting into laughter upon recognizing the item. "It's a California license plate...dated 1985." He showed it to Shadow who reacted with a wag of the tail. "Nothing foreign about it at all, except for you finding it here," he said, through another burst of laughter. "We made it to California, buddy, and without the reindeer."

Adam figured someone left it as a playful reminder, indicating to future hikers that they had, indeed, crossed the state line. Possibly, they had attached it to a tree before man or Mother Nature removed it. Initially, he considered keeping it as a memento but instead left it propped against a tree trunk for the next passerby's wonderment. He tethered Shadow to the leash. "Off we go, my friend."

He couldn't have asked for better weather thus far...seventies in the daytime...fifties at night. It appeared to have an impact on Shadow as he determinedly kept his nose to the ground, picking up the path running parallel to the creek they had traveled the previous day. No question his energy level had risen, Adam noted, as indicated by his sturdy pull on the leash.

They had traveled at least a quarter of a mile further up the hillside when Shadow took a left turn across a clearing toward a stand of trees fronted by a large live oak. He came to an abrupt stop aside the tree, then paced back and forth in front of it, before dropping to all fours. He tucked in his ears and tail and began to whimper.

"What is it, boy?" Adam asked, taking a knee by his side. The lab answered with more whimpers. Above, leaves rustled in the trees, as if they were whispering a secret to them.

Adam laid the leash on the ground, took a few steps back, and scanned the surroundings. Nothing appeared out of the ordinary. He again took a knee and stroked the lab's head. "What is it, buddy?" he repeated, prompting another whimper. Shadow's eyes remained fixed on the oak. Puzzled by the animal's behavior, he began to circle the tree's hefty trunk, bringing into view a sight that at once sucked right out of him whatever high-altitude air he had left in him.

The tree was hollowed out with a sizable surface hole to show for it. The opening was covered by a wire mesh and filled with what looked to be a mix of thick moss and a tar substance. He ripped off the wire covering stapled to the tree, exposing the filling of moss and tar. Grabbing handfuls of the stuff, he tossed it aside. The action gave vent to a foul smell he was all too familiar with, underscoring that what he was seeing was real, not another fiction of the mind. Gradually, the source of the odor emanating from the lengthy cavity was revealed. It was a sleeping bag. Bracing for what came next, Adam pulled the sleeping bag out partway, unzipped the top of the bag, disclosing the head of a man whose temple was marked by a bullet hole. His mind flashed back to the photo his client had provided him. It was Jeb Lanigan, alright. His face had not appreciably decomposed, leading him to conclude his death was recent.

Adam zipped the sleeping bag closed, replaced it in the trunk, and refilled the cavity with the mixture of moss and tar he had removed moments earlier. He next fetched the first aid kit from his backpack and removed a roll of medical tape. He tore off several strips of it and attached them to the ends of the wire mesh, which he attached to the tree. To support the covering, he snatched a small piece of nearby granite from the ground and with it hammered any staples not removed or damaged by the ripping off of the mesh back into the tree. It was a temporary fix, but it would have to do, since he had no tools at hand. When finished, he took a seat on the ground next to his companion with the forlorn look on his face and listened to the winds whipping through the trees.

"You know, Shadow, I once attended a lecture on forest therapy recommended by a former boss of mine," he said, stroking the dog's back. "The speaker explained to us that time spent in a forest featuring a fairly thick canopy of fully developed trees with a stream running through it, just like this one, engages a person's senses. It makes them less likely to suffer emotional strain. Well, it doesn't look like that forest therapy angle is working at the moment, does it?"

A somber mood had settled over them when at once it was vanquished by the sharp sound of a piece of bark being stripped from the trunk of the oak tree, followed in turn by a distinct, distant thud.

Rifle fire!

Adam grabbed the leash and pulled Shadow behind the oak alongside him, placing the tree between them and the direction of the gunfire. Two more rounds from the rifle chipped bark off the tree's above-ground roots not more than a foot from where they huddled. He recalled from his past military training the formula for determining the distance between a shooter and a target. "That's right, Fraley, bullets travel faster than sound," his sergeant informed him. "Snipers love it." One second of interval from the hit to the distant thud equals approximately six hundred yards...a half-second, three hundred yards. Adam estimated the differential as closer to one second for the first three rounds. Considering the distance and the number of obstacles in the line of sight, the guy was a gifted marksman, he reasoned.

The commotion stirred Shadow into a barking frenzy. "Be still, buddy," he said to the canine, placing his hand over the dog's snout to help quiet him.

Their position behind the tree was a precarious one...a temporary refuge at best. Despite the scattered stands of trees that stood as obstacles to the shooter, they were hunkered down in a mostly open area. They needed to get to the thicker clusters of trees and many boulders lining the stream that would provide them more protective cover. The challenge was crossing the twenty yards of open field required to reach there. Luckily, the lay of the land did offer them a path. Two elongated, narrow knolls, three feet in height and spaced ten feet apart spanned nearly the entire distance.

"Come on, Shadow," he said, taking a firm hold of his companion's leash and pointing across the way. "We have to get to those trees over there." He lowered himself into a crouching stance and with the dog in tow scrambled as fast as he could in a duck-walk manner the length of the first knoll. Facing them at this point was the ten feet of bare, leveled ground leading to the second knoll. "Gotta hurry with this stretch," he said to the lab. "This time I'm going alone...better he has only one target at a time." Adam let loose the leash. "Stay...stay," he commanded, pointing to the ground. Shadow dropped to all fours as Adam took a sprinter's stance and instantly raced to the cover of the second knoll. Close on his heels, a piece of turf ripped from the ground, the impact followed by a distant thud.

He turned his attention to Shadow who was primed to follow. He raised his hand to the dog. "Stay," he said, knowing an overt pattern or rhythm to their movements was a gift to a calculating killer. He imagined the shooter looking down his gunsight with his finger pressed against the trigger.

An eerie quiet settled over the scene, underscoring the old notion that when gunfire sounds, all other sounds cease. He waited a full minute before clapping his hands. "Now!" he said in a lowered voice, prompting Shadow to sprint to his side, a patch of turf exploding several feet behind him. "Good boy. You're too quick for him," he gushed, patting him on the head.

They moved into the thickets of trees that provided them cover on their path down the hillsides. A short while later, five more rounds, one right after the other, ricocheted through the tall timber. It was a stark reminder they were not out of the woods, nor did they wish to be at the moment.

Based on the firing pattern thus far, Adam figured the shooter was using a bolt-action rifle with five-round clips. The latest hit-thud interval indicated the guy was gaining on them, somewhere within two to three hundred yards of their location. He peeked from behind a tree and saw in the distance a familiar off-road vehicle approaching from across the opposite side of the creek.

Cruel.

The inevitable crept into his mind, as he urged Shadow along on their downward rush. They had reached the waterfall section of the creek where they had camped the previous night. The trees at this location thinned out considerably, once again leaving them vulnerable.

He tugged at Shadow's leash. "This way, buddy. We've got to take the rocky path if we're to retreat any further."

They rushed toward the large granite rocks bordering the stream, igniting another rapid round of rifle fire. Two of the bullets could be heard whistling past them, while another three chipped off chunks of the boulder they had taken refuge behind. The rock formations along the creek allowed them another hundred yards of safe passage downstream. At that juncture, their options took a precipitous drop as the boulders thinned out much like the trees had earlier. Great hunting territory for a sniper from here on out, Adam observed, and they still had three-quarters of a mile to go to reach the abandoned cabin and his rental car.

Minutes passed before five additional rounds ripped chunks of rock off the boulder. This time there was no interval between the firing and the impacting, signaling their tormentor was close at hand. He was making good use of his off-road vehicle, Adam gauged. The volley was followed by a loud, lacerating laugh that carried down the hillside. "What we have going on here is a glorious instant replay," Cruel bellowed.

It all came into focus for Adam. Lanigan had not been dead for long when they stumbled upon him...maybe three days. The likelihood was that he had somehow become aware of the drug trafficking taking place in the area and let it be known to the wrong people. So, what do the traffickers do? Send out their assassin to make sure the news travels no further. Perhaps Lanigan was caught alone in the hills while foraging for food or simply going for a bath in the creek. Chances are Shadow was with him when they were sighted, just like he and the lab were spotted a short time ago. And what about the lab? How did he escape his master's fate?

Adam looked at Shadow who was stretched out on the ground looking back at him with a quizzical look on his cocked face as if asking "What's next?" He suddenly realized it was the same question confronting Lanigan trapped in the same predicament. And now he came to recognize Lanigan's response. He had set Shadow free...took his leash and collar and commanded his charge to leave, knowing the canine's chance for survival would be greatly enhanced if he was not slowed by his owner. Yes, that's what led to him and Shadow crossing paths as he walked back from the waterfall the other day. The dog had been wandering the woods, probably for a couple of days, his instinct to hang close to his master, despite his command.

Five more rounds ripped shards of rock off the boulder. Cruel was playing with his prey, Adam reckoned, milking every ounce of perverse pleasure he could before executing the kill shots. Why not have some fun before he ran short on ammo? After all, it was not like he had an unlimited supply of it. Still, the fact was they had no weapon to offset his. All he had to do was charge them...flush them from behind the rock to finish them off.

"See those pine cones on that tree limb behind you?" the shooter hollered out.

Adam saw them but was not about to acknowledge the fact.

Instead, he took a quick peek from behind the boulder to confirm the sniper had his binoculars out.

Seconds later another series of shots rang out, peeling five of the cones off the cluster Cruel was referring to, leaving three remaining. There was that sequence of five again, Adam noted.

"Well, this is a fine mess we're in," he said to the lab.

"Woof."

"Why are you yawning? Humans are known to do that when they get anxious. Same with you?"

"Woof-woof," came the quick reply.

"Yeah, you and me both."

His thoughts drifted to his family and the promise he had made them long ago to call the cops whenever a case threatened to turn violent, an option that was not in play at the moment.

He rummaged through his backpack, searching for a pen he recalled dumping into it back at the hotel. After a rush of scattering and sifting, he located it. He next tore off the blank side of a boxed container of medical tape. On it, he wrote a message to his wife and daughter. He then took some of the tape and attached it to Shadow's collar.

"Make your move!" Cruel shouted out in his venomous tone, "or I'll make one for you."

Adam removed the leash from the lab. "Time for you to leave, my friend. You're too quick for him. I'm not. Go ahead...go."

Shadow dug his paws into the turf and let go a low "woof" directly at him.

Adam gave him a shove and at once regretted it. He sighed his discomfort. "You don't want to go this time, is that it?"

Another "woof" and the lab inched closer to him.

"Look, my friend, we have three options...cut and run, give up —which is really no option—or stand and fight." He considered the choices for a moment. "On second thought, there is a fourth."

He snatched the dog's leash and attached it back to him, threading it under his collar several times, so as not to let it become a flying impediment. He then took hold of the collar and directed Shadow's attention to a boulder on the opposite side of the creek nearly twenty-five yards upstream, where a wide-brimmed canvas hat could be seen bobbing up and down behind it. Several yards behind the shooter stood his off-road vehicle.

Adam felt the pull of the collar and the burst of energy in the lab upon recognizing the target.

In as mocking a tone as he could muster, Adam shouted out to the shooter. "So far, Cruel, all I've learned is that your aim leaves a lot to be desired."

It worked. Four more rounds dug into the boulder, spraying bits of it in every direction.

Come on...one more.

A fifth shot ripped into the rock. "Go!" Adam yelled to the lab, releasing his hand from the collar.

Shadow bolted ahead, followed by Adam. The canine used the smooth stones protruding from the creek as stepping stones in his lightning dash to the target. Adam followed ten yards behind him, splashing through the water. He spotted Cruel hurriedly snapping a new magazine into his rifle and raising it toward his shoulder the moment Shadow launched himself at the assassin from the top of the boulder the gunman had been operating behind. A shot rang out the instant the canine barreled into the shooter, knocking the weapon from his hands. Cruel scrambled to retrieve it but Adam had arrived in time to kick it out of his reach.

"Here...maybe this will improve your aim even more," he said, grabbing the guy by the hair and spraying flush into his face a blast of the bear repellent he was carrying in his other hand. "Aargh!" Cruel wailed, loud enough to awaken a hibernating bear.

Adam quickly turned his attention to Shadow who was sitting on his haunches in a deflated state, as though the air had been knocked out of him. His initial concern that the animal may have been wounded by the errant shot turned out to be true. An abrasion on his side was seeping blood. While Cruel wailed away, Adam snatched from his emergency kit several gauze pads to apply pressure to the area to stop Shadow's bleeding. He next applied a layer of antibiotic ointment to the wound before bandaging it.

Cruel continued his moaning, as he vigorously rubbed his eyes in a futile effort to clear them.

"Shut the hell up!" Adam snapped. Walking over to the once braggadocious hitman, he grabbed him by the arms and dragged him to the edge of the creek. "Stick your face in it. Maybe it will help." He took the occasion to pat him down, searching for the keys to his off-road vehicle. He found them in a front pocket.

"I'll get you for this, Fraley," Cruel roared.

"Interesting that you know my name," Adam responded, grabbing the guy's rifle.

"You'd better kill me while you have the chance," he warned, before dropping his face into the creek to help clear them.

"You are in no position to be warning anybody, you jackass!" Adam replied, shoving the guy's face deeper into the water.

On his walk back to check on Shadow, he spotted Cruel's magazine pouch on the ground. It was empty. Undoubtedly, the magazine he had hurriedly loaded into the rifle was the one he was saving for his final charge.

Adam turned his attention to Shadow. For the first time, he saw fear in the animal's eyes. The dog was anxiously angling his head around, attempting to locate the source of his pain. "Good boy," he said, pouring water across his head and into his mouth. "You ready to get out of here?"

"Woof," came his answer in a weakened tone.

They walked a short distance to the off-road vehicle. Adam placed the rifle into the back seat and, after letting Shadow into the passenger side, hopped into the front seat. He reached over and removed from the dog's collar the message to his family he had attached to it. He paused momentarily to consider what to do about Cruel. Killing him was not an option, and without readily available restraints such as handcuffs or rope, it'd be tough to do anything further. Besides, he wanted to get Shadow to a clinic ASAP.

"Hold on, buddy," he said, igniting the engine. "We're about to go rocking and rolling down this hill."

CHAPTER EIGHT

REACHING THE INTERSECTION OF THE CREEK AND THE backwoods hiking trail he first came in on, Adam took a left, fully aware that hanging a right would have taken him to the abandoned cabin and his Jeep. Though still early in the day, time was of the essence, underscored by the blood seeping through Shadow's bandage. He needed immediate attention.

On his drive-by of Solitaire, he caught sight of Walt's pickup and the day laborers' van. "So far, I have yet to see a single customer at that store, other than me," he mumbled to himself.

Back on the road to Reno, he kept a lookout for strip shopping centers and roadside signboards listing tenants in the hope of finding a veterinarian's office. He was about to stop and ask someone if they knew of a nearby vet when he spotted a sign for one. Better yet, it was an animal hospital.

Adam parked the off-road vehicle and took his companion in his arms. "We're going to get you some help, buddy," he said to the lab. A sign in the lobby of the clinic pointed him in the direction of the canine wing.

"Hold on there!" a stern-faced, matronly woman called out to him from behind the Registration Desk, as he hurried by. "We do have a priority system in place here, you know."

"You do?" he responded innocently.

"Yes—like, if it bleeds, it leads," she said through pursed lips.

Adam looked about the service area. "Oh, I must have missed it. Is that posted somewhere?"

"No, it's in the hospital's written policies, which I would be happy to show you."

"When you say 'if it bleeds,' you mean the animal, like this one here that's bleeding."

The woman glanced at Shadow. "Yes, of course—certainly not the owner," she replied with a condescending chuckle.

"That's good to know, because if it did refer to the owner, then I would be first in line, since right about now I have blood shooting out of my eyes, in case you didn't notice."

About this time, a guy with a big girth, wide smile, and wearing a white lab coat, stepped out of the background with impeccable timing into the middle of the testy exchange. "Well, what have we here?" he said at the sight of Shadow's bloodied bandage.

"He got swiped by a deranged animal," Adam said, figuring any mention of a bullet wound might spark legal delays.

"A deranged animal...okay," the staff member absentmindedly said, his interest totally on the bandage he was taking a peek under. "What's his name?"

"Shadow...Are you a vet?"

"Yes...you'll need to fill out one of those registration forms piled on the desk there if you've not already done so."

"No, I have not."

"Okay, while you're doing that, I'll take a look at him in the exam room."

Adam handed over the lab. Avoiding eye contact with his newfound nemesis, lest he lose whatever patience he had left, he filled out the form and took a seat to await the diagnosis. Fifteen minutes later, the vet was back. "We'll need to clean out the wound thoroughly and probably give him a few stitches. He should be fine. Are you from here?"

"No...Florida. I'm here on business for a few days."

"Well, you can have the stitches removed elsewhere with no trouble, if that's your preference."

"Doctor, is it possible to leave him here overnight? I have pressing business that requires me to be out on the road. I'd feel more comfortable knowing he is here."

"Sure. It might be best if we monitor him overnight, anyway, though it will cost you a few extra bucks."

"No problem...Can I see him?"

"Yes, follow me, and by the way, here's my card in case you need to get in touch."

He was directed to a large crate housing Shadow who was resting on all fours. As soon as the lab saw him approaching, he was on his feet attempting a little happy dance. Adam dropped to a knee to face him, sliding his fingers through the crate's bars for the lab to lick.

"Say, buddy, you're going to be in here a while longer. I want you to know they're going to take good care of you...okay?" he said, withdrawing his fingers.

The lab cocked his head, looking at him with puzzlement.

"Okay?" Adam repeated.

"Woof," he responded with a tone of resignation, his woeful eyes suggesting he'd much rather be roaming the hills.

———

By noon, Adam was back at his hotel room and on the phone with his wife in Tampa. "I need your help on three matters, babe, and I need them within an hour, if at all possible."

"You sound hurried, or should I say harried?"

"Both apply at this juncture."

"I'll see what I can do...what are they?"

"The first relates to a woman by the name of Alicia Hastings. Supposedly, she lived in the San Francisco area around a half-century ago. She was a descendent of a man by the name of Lansford Hastings, the guy for whom the foundation was named.

She may have been a granddaughter or great-granddaughter of his."

"Anything in particular you need to know?"

"Simply, whether there is any record of her existence."

"Hmmm...interesting. Next?"

"I need to know who this Nevada license plate number belongs to," he said, rattling off the number.

"Got it...and the last one?"

"I'd like for you to get hold of our contact person in the FBI office there...Jim Alexander. See if he can give me a contact name in their Reno office. I plan on visiting them this afternoon."

"Sounds like things are getting serious way out west."

"They're way past serious."

"Do you want to elaborate on that?"

"Not this minute. I'm too pressed for time, I'm afraid."

"No problem...the details can come later."

"One last matter. It looks as though I'll have to spend an extra day or two here on the case. Tell Noelle I should be home in plenty of time for her campus tours."

"I will, and don't worry. She'll be fine with any delay, as long as we don't scrap them altogether."

"Good...I'll await your call back."

"Adam?"

"Yes?"

"Be careful. I sense a seriousness that tells me you may be in harm's way."

FIGURING it would take his wife the full hour to do the digging, Adam decided to conduct some research of his own. Forthwith, he hustled down to the hotel parking lot to Cruel's off-road vehicle to comb through it for items that might be relevant to the case. He started with the glove compartment and at once hit on a couple of items of obvious interest...a receipt from Jack's Outdoor Sporting Goods store and a pocket calendar, no doubt belonging to him.

Thumbing through the most recent weeks, several entries stood out, a number having to do with the "professor."

"Nosy neighbor—check with professor, feral pigs—check with professor, travel expenses—check with professor." It was as though the guy couldn't make a move without running it by the professor... aka his boss, Adam presumed. He was confident in eliminating Walt and the day laborers as holders of the title. There was nothing professorial about them.

One other scribbling tweaked his interest. "Stash—deadwood—nosy stranger—check with professor." He reckoned the latter entry was referencing none other than he, intimating he was scheduled to receive the same fate as the new nosy neighbor Jeb Lanigan.

Adam pocketed the receipt and calendar and took a quick look around the remainder of the vehicle's interior, finding scattered gun magazines and several comic books. He checked the trunk last, discovering another batch of comic books. "Stress relievers while you're waiting around to knock somebody off," he remarked aloud. Finished with the inspection, he returned to his room to take a nap.

He was passing the hotel's front desk when he stopped to ask the clerk if he happened to know the location of the Reno Beacon. "Two blocks down the street we're on," he was told. "Two-story brick building...you can't miss it."

He may have needed a nap, but he couldn't pass up the opportunity to track down a possible lead such a short distance away; so, back out the front entrance he went and down the street he headed.

Upon entering the Beacon building, he asked the receptionist if a man by the name of Ned Garland was still on the staff. Her response was at once somewhat surprising and entirely gratifying. "He sure is. Would you like to speak with him?"

"Yes...please."

"Your name?"

"Adam Fraley."

"Can I tell him what this is about?"

"A story he wrote years ago."

She dialed an extension. "There's a man here by the name of Adam Fraley who would like to speak with you regarding a story you wrote years ago...yes, I'll tell him."

She hung up the phone. "He says he will meet you in the lobby."

Adam took a seat in one of four upholstered armchairs surrounding a narrow Indian rug spread across a dark hardwood floor. A minute later, Garland appeared, clad in denims and a flannel shirt. He was a wiry man with a lean face reflective of a guy who had led an active life chasing after Northern Nevada stories.

The two introduced themselves and took seats facing each other. "What can I do for you?" Garland asked in a soft voice that belied his sturdy exterior.

"I'm a private investigator from Florida working on a missing person case. During the course of it, I came across a guy named George Riley. I understand you did a feature story on him some twenty years ago. Does the name ring a bell?"

Garland looked aside and into the distance, his mind in rewind. "Yeah, I remember him...the professor."

"According to the article, he was fired from his tenured job at Valley State College due to a gambling addiction he developed, which caused him to miss an excessive number of classes."

"Right...an addiction to the game of solitaire, which puzzled many people at the time."

"It puzzles me," Adam said. "Other than it was played with a deck of cards, I never associated it with gambling, particularly in a casino setting."

"There are few rules on what someone can offer bets on in the gaming industry. An old saying in these parts goes like this, 'If you can think about it, you can bet on it, as long as a bookmaker believes there is a market for it.' Back in those days, several casinos in the Reno area offered solitaire wagering."

"How did it work?"

"You paid a set amount for a deck. If agreed to by the house, the amount represented the bet you were making. You then played the game while a casino worker stood by and watched. Some workers could watch you play multiple games at once if that was your choice. If you missed a move that you could have made, the game was declared over by the house. Otherwise, you went through the entire deck, one card at a time. You were paid according to the number of cards that ended up in your foundation piles, which could be more or less than your initial bet, if that means anything to you."

"It doesn't."

"Anyway, the game took up too much space on the tables for the amount of income it generated. Plus, the many computer versions now provide the public an easily accessible fix."

"Perhaps because I never played the game, I never understood its appeal," Adam confessed. "What makes a person want to compete against himself? One side of you always comes out a winner...is that it?"

"In the non-wagering version, you can derive a mental benefit —win or lose. Remember, the game was shown to be addictive to many people even before the betting aspect was added by the gambling houses. In the old casino version, you did not always come out a winner, so you weren't playing against yourself. You were playing against the house. As always, in order to get the buzz, you had to face the risk of losing. Therein rested casino solitaire's appeal...in the combining of the game and the gambling."

"To people like Riley."

"Yes, though it eventually led to his downfall and the loss of his wife, who left him over it. Needless to say, he came out of it a very bitter man, not to mention a much poorer one."

"Speaking of solitaire, do you know of a place up in the Sierra foothills that goes by that name?"

"What kind of place?"

"A strange one, for sure. It's a restored, stand-alone structure that serves as a sort of way station for random travelers. However, the road it's on—if you can call it that—appears to be nothing more than an abandoned trail."

Garland propped one of his legs on top of the other and clasped his hands behind his head, as though his interest had been tweaked.

"What you're describing sounds like one of the leftover toll houses from the previous century."

"Toll house?"

"Yep...that's what they were called. During the construction boom of the gold rush days, companies would build them along routes they expected to be designated as toll roads. Back then you could claim land, build on it, and it was yours. Sometimes their expectations were nothing more than guesswork as to the future locale of the planned routes. They turned out to be bad bets and a lot of the buildings were left abandoned, as a result of planners having jumped the gun. That must be the case with the one you are referring to. At one time, there must have been over a hundred of those toll houses built in this region, due to the Comstock Lode gold and silver deposits discovered near Virginia City, as well as other mining operations located in the foothills. Those were crazy days around here. Seemingly, the whole country was descending on Northern Nevada. Even Mark Twain got into the act, investing in mining ventures that ultimately went nowhere. He ended up doing what he did best...writing a column for a local newspaper."

"Yeah, like you say, the building I have in mind could be one of those leftover toll houses," Adam said, rising from his chair. "Well, I won't take up any more of your time. I thank you for your information."

"Good luck in your search," Garland said, getting to his feet to bid him farewell.

Adam hustled back to the hotel, pleased with not only the information he had garnered, but for the question not posed by the veteran newsman. "Is there a connection between your search for Riley and the toll house in the hills?" No doubt, given the details, it could have led to Garland inserting himself into the story with the potential of hijacking it. Nothing gets in the way of a scoop for a newsman or a clue to a detective.

Adam hustled back to his room and immediately collapsed on the bed, determined to get that nap, as brief as it might be.

TAMRA SAT AT HER DESK, reflecting on a hunch of hers. It stemmed from a notion of Adam's, instilled in him by his old boss Pete Peterson, that over a half of their cases could be solved without leaving the office. How so? By determining any connections between the major players in the case by working the phones. As she pointed out to him, not all of the players are present at the beginning. "Well, I'll amend that to say as they come on stage," he said. She had to admit there was truth to the notion. Discovering the hidden connections was often the key to solving the puzzle presented to them. As her husband liked to point out, "It saves a lot of gumshoeing."

The players she had in mind were Jeb Lanigan and George Riley.

She called Cal Taylor to ask if he knew how long Jeb worked as an independent financial advisor. "Oh, I'd say at least 15 years," he answered. "Was he always an independent advisor, or did he work for another outfit prior to becoming one?" Taylor thought for a moment. "No, he wasn't always an independent operator. If I recall right, he worked as a financial analyst for a bank, before going it alone," he replied with a degree of certainty. "Do you remember the name of the bank?" she asked. "Jeez, I'm not sure I can name it off hand," he said, delving further into his past. "It's one of those names, if I heard it, I would recognize it," he said. "Does the name Washoe State Bank ring a bell?" she asked. "That's it—Washoe State Bank!" She thanked him for the info. "Any news on Jeb?" he asked. "Nothing major to report yet," she said, again thanking him for his input.

So, Jeb worked at the Washoe State Bank at the same time the Hastings Foundation, one of their clients, was in operation, she concluded. What to make of it?

ADAM WOKE WITH A START, the loud buzz of the phone ending his shut-eye.

"Okay, I've come up with two hits and an incomplete, I guess you could say," his wife announced. "First of all, the license plate number belongs to Jeb Lanigan...surprised?"

"Can't say I am."

"Secondly, I contacted Jim Alexander, who, in turn, got in touch with the FBI office in Reno. He said an agent by the name of Lauren Staley will be expecting a visit from you sometime this afternoon," she said, reciting the address of the bureau office. "I gave Jim a general idea of what the case was all about."

"Good."

"Thirdly, I can't be definite as to whether the Alicia Hastings you were referring to actually existed. I conducted a quick check of all the obits for that period and there were far too many entries for the name to sort through in such a short time. It would take a complete genealogical search, I'm afraid, to determine if the person you have in mind existed. However, I did find a genealogical chart for Lansford Hastings and can tell you with certainty there was no Alicia Hastings listed."

"Another non-surprise."

"Regarding the Hastings Foundation. I dug a little deeper into the public records and they show the organization was issued a license to conduct charitable gaming activities, something the state of Nevada passed into law some time back for non-profits."

"Activities to bet on?"

"Yes, though the games were specifically limited to raffles, blackjack, poker, and bingo—no slot machines or roulette wheels."

"How long ago was the license issued?"

"Not long after the organization went into operation."

"Interesting—I'll have to give some thought to that one. Thanks, babe."

"Oh, and Adam, there is one other bit of information I came up with that should interest you."

"What's that?"

"I discovered that Jeb Lanigan, prior to his working as an independent financial advisor, worked as a financial analyst for a Reno bank, and not just any bank. Want to take a guess?"

"Washoe Bank?"

"The Hastings Foundation was up and running at the time he was working there?"

"Indeed. It may not amount to anything, but I thought I should bring it to your attention."

"Yeah, I'll have to ponder that one too. Meanwhile, how's everything on the home front?"

"Everything and everybody, including your daughter, is fine. We're just waiting for your return, so things can return to normal."

"As I've said many times in the past, my dear, when are things ever normal with Adam Fraley Private Investigations?"

———

ADAM SAT at his tiny hotel desk, propped his hand on his chin, and reflected first on the bank connection, following the call with his wife. As far as he knew, the job of a bank financial analyst was to track and analyze the institution's overall financial performance. They do not concern themselves with individual customer accounts. That's left for the underlings. If that was the case in this instance, the probability of a face-to-face interaction between Lanigan and a Hasting's Foundation representative making a routine deposit was low. That's not to say they could not have crossed paths on the bank's property in some happenstance contact. It's also possible, when Lanigan first entered the world of Solitaire, for the bank connection to be made by one of the parties involved, simply through a face recognition. One way or the other, whether the players were familiar with each other from bank interactions or not, it was the unearthing of the drug trafficking operation that ultimately led to Lanigan's death. Nonetheless, he would bring the connection to the FBI's attention.

As for the Hastings Foundation's acquisition of a charitable gaming license, Riley might have seen it as a convenient way to feed his gambling addiction, coming, as it was, on the heels of his firing. Yet, the idea he could convert Solitaire into some sort of casino operation at the time seemed ludicrous on the surface. He might have been a charlatan, but he was not a foolish one. Solitaire was far too isolated to serve as a brick-and-mortar gaming site. Maybe he had another location in mind, Adam ruminated, or was looking at it as a future online venture. However, from all outward appearances, the idea never got off the ground. No, it was all a passing fancy, so the professor turned to a far more lucrative endeavor, more in keeping with Solitaire's setting.

CHAPTER NINE

ONE DAY, ADAM WOULD MEET AN FBI AGENT WHO DIDN'T FIT the department's image. This was not the day. Lauren Staley's velvety voice came across as sensuous when they had spoken on the phone earlier. In person, she was the image of smartness, from her upright posture, and clear, narrow face, to her rimless glasses behind which burned intelligent blue eyes. She was clothed in a ginger-colored pantsuit that nicely matched her light brown hair knotted at the back.

"By the way...call me Lauren," she said softly, belying her steely demeanor. "We like to maintain an informality around here as best we can."

"Make it Adam for me," he said in return.

"So, there's a dead body stuffed in a hollowed-out tree in the Sierra foothills," she stated from behind a tidy desk.

"Yes, like I said, in an oak tree by the creek, not far from the waterfall I mentioned."

She picked up the phone and dialed a number. "The sheriff's department has an aviation enforcement unit that covers the Sierra foothills," she said in an aside to him. "They need to be notified."

Adam heard a distant mechanized voice on the other end say, "Yes?" after two rings.

"Yes, this is Lauren Staley over at the FBI office in Reno. Is Sheriff Collins in? We have an emergency situation I'd like to discuss with him...thank you."

Lauren cupped the phone to deliver a message to Adam. "They're tracking him down...you said you're driving the shooter's vehicle...is the rifle still in it?"

"Yes."

"Loaded?"

"Yes. I wanted to leave it as is until it could be examined."

"Okay, we'll make sure to take a look at it right away," she said, grabbing a pen to make note of it. "And the dog is in the hospital... how's he doing?"

"Fine, when I last left him."

"I'm somewhat familiar with that area of the foothills you are describing. The creek you are referring to is called Crawford Creek...hello sheriff? Sorry to interrupt your business, but I've just been notified by a man sitting across from me that there is a dead body of a male stuffed into a hollowed-out oak tree in the Sierra foothills. Apparently, he died from a shot to the head. The man who discovered him was in turn attacked by an armed male, but managed to escape. It's possible the killer is still on the loose. We're still in the process of collecting the details. What I'm wondering is, if you could send a unit up there to check out the scene...where exactly? He says the tree is located near Crawford Creek, about fifty yards from the small waterfall, if you know where that is...you do...thanks much, sheriff. We'll be heading up that way ourselves, as soon as I get off the phone."

Lauren turned her attention to Adam. "He's sending an air unit to the scene right now."

"You want me to follow you up?"

"No, you can ride with us."

She picked up the phone again and dialed an extension number. "Jeff, can you step into my office? I've got an assignment for you."

Moments later, a strapping young man with a shock of black

hair, a chiseled face, a firm jaw, and alert hazel eyes entered the room.

"Jeff, this is Adam Fraley, the private investigator from Florida I was telling you about," she said, by way of introduction, prompting the two to exchange nods. "I'd like you to ride along with us on a trip into the foothills to check out an apparent murder. I'll brief you along the way." She next turned to Adam. "And I'd like for you to retrieve that rifle for safe keeping before we leave."

"Will do," Adam said.

"While you're doing that, Jeff and I will change into our field gear. We'll then be off and running."

————

"You've worked with Jim Alexander in Tampa?" Lauren asked from behind the driver's wheel.

"Yes, in a couple of cases over the years," Adam responded from a rear seat. "How about you?"

"We were classmates at the FBI Academy."

"This guy who was killed...he was a client of yours?" Jeff asked from the passenger side.

"No, he wasn't a client. A close friend of his hired me to find him when he went missing."

"That note in Cruel's pocket calendar linking the stash and deadwood...what is the chance of him stuffing the drug haul in another hollowed-out tree?" Lauren asked as she guided the FBI van up the last stretch of road leading to Solitaire. "It falls in line with his 'nosy neighbor—deadwood' entry, not to mention the 'nosy stranger—deadwood' one," she said, glancing around to flash him a quick grin.

"It's certainly within the realm of possibility," Adam answered. "The guy may think he's hit on a convenient tactic with the hollowed-out tree idea. I'm not sure there are enough hollowed-out trees in the Sierra Nevada range to satisfy his bloodlust, however."

"You say he could still be wandering the hills?" Jeff asked. "Unarmed?"

"Can't say for sure. Guy like that feels naked without one, so he'll likely find a replacement weapon once he gets his act together. Right now, he's probably loping around the hills, looking a lot like Big Foot."

"What is the chance of him finding one at this place called Solitaire we're headed to?" Lauren speculated.

"It's a possibility," Adam said. "They have lots of inventory, not all of it on display," he pointed out. "Chances are there is a weapon or two tucked away somewhere on the property."

"What are the odds a crew of wildlife adventurers will mistake him for Sasquatch and haul his butt off to some exotic museum first," Jeff cracked.

"None, we're going to get first crack at him...or he at us," Adam countered, catching via the rearview mirror a small smile forming on Lauren's face, as they rounded the final turn on their approach to the property.

"Whatever business they're in, it doesn't appear to be flourishing today," Jeff observed, noting a single vehicle parked out front.

"Why is it you want to stop here?" Lauren asked Adam.

"I've got an item to pick up I noticed on the shelf the other day when I was in here, plus I thought you'd like to check out the store."

"I've seen this place before while on my hiking trips," Lauren said. "I never paid it much attention. Now I could kick myself for having become so oblivious to it."

"A forgotten place in time," Jeff said.

Lauren eased the van to a stop next to the pickup, and the three entered the store.

If seeing Adam again was not enough to ruin Walt's day, seeing him accompanied by two armed FBI agents was sure to cause him a ton of concern. Nary a word emanated from the guy's mouth as the three commenced to peruse the shelves.

Adam stepped to the cleaning products section and pulled from a shelf a large glass jar labeled "Laundry Detergent."

"Found what I wanted," he announced to the agents who joined him at the checkout counter. He handed the container to Walt who eyed him hesitantly, setting off a round of eye-tag among the three visitors and the manager.

"Where did you find this?" Walt asked, as if it wasn't something officially part of the inventory...perhaps put there by mistake.

"On the shelf over there. How much for it?" he asked, spurring Walt along.

"Four bucks," he reluctantly replied. Adam doled out four dollars, which Walt deposited in a cash drawer, precipitating another waiting game. "I'd appreciate a receipt," Adam said, when seeing the manager was not inclined to offer one. A brief stare-down ensued, before Walt withdrew from the cash drawer a receipt book, filling one out and handing it to him.

"There you go Mr. Fraley," he said testily.

"Have a nice day," Adam said in return, igniting an additional round of eye-tag before the three walked out of the store.

"What was that all about?" Lauren asked back in the van.

"It was about this," Adam said, handing the jar to Jeff in the front seat. The agent held the container up, observing the off-white powder inside it.

"Is this what I think it may be?" He unscrewed the top to apply the smell and taste test. "Yeah, that's nose candy alright."

"Why would they have a jar of it sitting in plain sight on the shelf?" Lauren asked.

"A good question," Adam answered. "I'm guessing there are multiple jars of it hidden away on the property somewhere...an amount equal to what was exposed by the hogs."

"Still, why even put one jar on the shelf?" Lauren followed.

"Who knows," Adam continued. "Could be it was placed there by mistake by one of their underlings with a bad command of the language. Crooks do make mistakes, especially when they have had it their way for years, and become complacent. My guess is that during the transfer of the stash, one of the labeled jars they filled with the stuff was inadvertently placed on the shelf. That's what Walt's reaction was telling me. It shouldn't have been put there in the first place."

"So, each side now knows what the other side is aware of," Lauren said. "Does that make sense?"

"Makes perfect sense to me," Adam responded with a grin.

"Can you imagine someone trying to clean their clothes with this stuff?" Jeff said, still eyeing the coke.

"There have been dealers who've tried to dump it in the wash during raids," Lauren said.

"Everyone's got to have plan B, no matter what business you're in...right?" Jeff joshed, setting the jar aside.

"What you say about it being accidentally placed on the shelf may be true, Adam, but, if the remaining jars are hidden in there, we would need a search warrant to legally determine if it is true. Even that jar Jeff is holding would be ruled inadmissible without such a warrant," Lauren posited.

"Why?" Adam countered. "A legitimate customer...me... purchased a canister of laundry detergent and turned it over to the FBI when he discovered it was funny stuff." Adam reached into his pocket. "Here's your proof," he added, handing Jeff the receipt.

The van's radio buzzed. Lauren placed it on speaker. "Agent Staley...this is Sheriff Collins. We've located the victim. The crime scene crew is here conducting an examination. Are you headed this way?"

"Yes, we should be up there within the hour."

They drove to the abandoned cabin, pulling to a stop next to Adam's rental. He checked the vehicle's condition, finding it in the same condition as he left it...a mild surprise, considering the vulnerable location.

"Nice cabin," Lauren commented. "The guy put some work into it. Have you checked the interior?"

"Yes. There are a few furnishings scattered about, and that's about it."

"Like someone has yet to fully settle in," Jeff suggested.

"Right," Adam said. "He was still in the hunting and gathering stage."

"We all set?" Lauren asked, drawing nods from her two

companions. "Okay, you lead the way," she said to Adam with a wave of the hand.

Leading the way was a task best served by Shadow, Adam reckoned. How the lab loved hearing that command coming from him...tail wagging...paws prancing in place...eyes anticipating. Instead, with two armed FBI agents by his side, he was headed up the slopes for the second time in a day that was not even half over, weaving around tall timber, rocks, and shrubs, all the while keeping a lookout for hollowed-out trees and his buddy Sasquatch scouring the woods. Needless to say, they took their time considering Adam's recent high-altitude episode he had related to them on the ride up. He assured them he was up for a second climb.

"These hills feel like they have eyes," Jeff commented as they made their way up. "Think of the stories they must have to tell... enough to fill several thousand books, I would say."

"No question, considering what they've witnessed through the years, much of it related to the westward expansion," Lauren added. "Lots of history made here...some good, some not so good."

"Or, on a smaller scale, what they are about to witness," Adam suggested.

Another hour of climbing turned up no additional hollowed-out trees. Gradually, the crime scene came into view up ahead. A large sheriff's chopper could be seen resting on the meadow approximate to the infamous oak tree. Several deputies were milling about.

———

"Hey, Lauren, it's been a while since we've crossed paths!" the sheriff called out to her upon their approach. A baby-faced man, he had the build of a lumberjack that was appropriate for the locale and the occasion, Adam observed.

"We've got the deceased victim loaded up," the sheriff continued. "What's his story...do you know?"

"He was a close friend of a client of private investigator Adam Fraley here who has been working on the case," she explained, motioning toward Adam. "Apparently, the victim became aware of a drug trafficking operation in this area and perhaps intended to blow the lid on it when he was taken out."

"But he was not one of the traffickers?" the sheriff asked.

"We don't believe so. He was evidently a bystander who, like I mentioned, was probably close to spilling the beans, or so the drug traffickers likely assumed."

"You got a liaison who can keep in contact with us on this? It's something we need to be updated on, considering it's also under our jurisdiction."

"I'll appoint one right now, sheriff...Jeff Conley," Lauren said, pointing to the agent. "In fact, if you have room on that chopper of yours, he can accompany you on your ride back and bring you up to date on what we know so far."

"Hey, pretty lady, you've got yourself a deal there. We've got room if he doesn't mind sitting next to a corpse," the sheriff cracked, flashing a smile Jeff's way.

"Can you also give him a ride back to our office?"

"No problem. What's next on your agenda?"

"We're going to head back down the hill and maybe take a second look at an abandoned cabin that may have belonged to the victim."

"Good hunting!" the sheriff shouted with a parting wave, as he and Jeff climbed into the aircraft.

They stepped back and watched the helicopter lift off. The chuff-chuff-chuff of its rotating blades filled the air, as the chopper rose up and over the hillside.

"The man wanted to get away from it all and now he has for good," Adam said, as the aircraft disappeared into the valley beyond. "How ironic. I've been told the primary motivation for people to move off the grid is their concern over what the future holds for them. If only he knew."

"Have you ever given thought to a life in the wilds, Adam?"

"In my younger days, I played with the idea, though I looked at it as more of a challenge than an escape. How about you?"

"I'm much too acclimated to modern conveniences."

He turned his gaze from the sky to Lauren. "Well, pretty lady. Shall we begin the trek back down?"

She chuckled. "The sheriff is very much old school in case you didn't notice."

Before heading down, Adam strolled over to the emptied oak tree, Lauren following in his footsteps. His gaze fell on the barks of wood ripped from the tree's trunk and roots by the rifle fire from earlier in the day.

"Who's behind all of this, Adam?" Lauren asked, her eyes fixed on the one particularly visible bruise to the oak's side. "Do you have any idea?"

Adam turned to her. "That guy, Walt, the one who waited on us over at the Solitaire store..."

"Yes," she interjected in anticipation.

"He addressed me by my last name. There is only one person associated with Solitaire to whom I gave my last name and it wasn't Walt."

"And who was that?"

"The professor."

"The guy Cruel kept referring to in his calendar?"

"Yes...if he looks like a professor, talks like a professor, and carries himself like a professor, he's likely to be tagged as one."

"Who is this fellow you speak of?"

"His name is George Riley. He's the head man for an organization called the Western Historical Research Society."

"How'd you come across him?"

"I was looking for someone who might have knowledge of Solitaire and ended up visiting this historical society office, figuring someone there might have a clue. I ended up speaking to Riley, asking if he knew of the place. It turns out he knew quite a bit, including the fact its operation is funded by an outfit called the Hastings Foundation. What he didn't tell me was that he, himself, was the director of the foundation."

"And it serves as a front for the traffickers," she surmised.

"You got it."

"You mentioned in your briefing to me over the phone this

morning, that there was a bank connection between the deceased and the Hastings Foundation."

"Yes, as I said, they were both connected to the Washoe State Bank—Lanigan as an upper-echelon employee—a financial analyst — and the Hastings Foundation as a customer. However, the more I think about it, I've come to believe there was no direct interaction between the two, only incidental ones, if any at all."

"Like walking past each other in the lobby."

"Yes—or to and from the parking lot. It's entirely possible Lanigan went to his death completely unaware of the Hasting Foundation's existence or its hand in his demise."

"Well, our agency can check the financial records of the Foundation and match them against the bank records to see if there are any significant discrepancies."

"The eye test says there must be. You saw the inside of the store. Did it look like a wealth-generating business to you?"

"Maybe, they do a great delivery service," she joshed.

"Oh, I'm sure they do a great delivery service, but it isn't for turnips. The professor wouldn't stand for it. His product of choice is a real money generator."

"Perhaps we should pay him a visit."

"Definitely, but first we have to make it back down this hill," he said, nodding to the route they traveled up. As you know, this will be the second roundtrip for me in as many days. Who was it that said that insanity was doing the same thing over and over and expecting a different result?"

"That would be Einstein, I believe, though I'm not sure it applies in this instance."

"You're the experienced hiker," Adam said, taking the first steps back down. "Going up or down...which is easier?"

"You might be surprised at the answer," she said, sidestepping a granite rock in her path. "Most people consider going downhill as gravity helping you out. However, there are other factors that come into play...age...terrain...length of stride...altitude. Going downhill is harder on your knees since you're continually using them as a brake to maintain your speed and balance," she explained between breaths. "All of those factors I mentioned help determine the ease and impact on the body, whether you're going up or down."

"You left out one factor in determining speed," he pointedly said.

"What's that?"

"Sniper fire."

"Right...that will slow you for sure...and me. Or it might quicken one's pace, as the case may be."

"Say, do you mind if we take a quick detour?" he asked.

"Detour? What's up?"

"There's another crime scene I'd like to check out that's close by."

Adam led her to the creek and across it to the boulder that Cruel turned into a playpen.

"And where were you and Shadow positioned at this point?"

Adam pointed downstream. "On the opposite side of the creek, about twenty-five yards down, where that cluster of boulders is located."

He lowered his gaze to the turf around them. "There should be several handfuls of shell casings scattered on the ground here, as well as an empty magazine or two."

"I see them," Lauren said, stooping to collect a handful of the shell casings, along with the empty magazines, slipping them into her pocket. "These could come in handy. The ballistics people can verify if it was the same weapon used in the Lanigan killing."

Adam strode about, recalling the incident, specifically the shot he now was convinced was intended for him and not Shadow.

"So, Cruel ended up with his face in the water."

"Yes. As I mentioned in my briefing to you before, my mind was on the dog. He was wounded, and I needed to get him some help fast. Otherwise, I would have hauled him in to the authorities, particularly if I had had something with which to restrain him."

He spotted two of the bloody gauze pads he had used on Shadow lying on the ground. He picked them up and shoved them into his pocket.

Lauren briefly laid a hand on his shoulder. "Understandable, Adam."

"Do you have any idea which way he may have headed after your encounter?" she asked.

"No, though considering his condition, he likely went downhill rather than uphill."

They walked downstream a short distance and crossed back over the creek. "I hope you don't mind getting your shoes a little wet," he said.

"I thought about slipping them off for the first crossing, but hey, I do have some trooper in me."

"See those three pine cones hanging on that tree limb behind the boulder there?" he asked.

"I see them."

"There once were eight there, before Cruel picked off five of them."

"Doing a little showboating, was he?"

"He was proficient with his weapon, alright. Thankfully, he just wasn't interested nearly as much in counting, as he was in killing."

They strolled back to the open field to continue their trek down the hillside.

———

"ALL IN ALL, I'd say we made it down faster than we made it up," Lauren declared on their reaching the cross trail where both stopped to catch their breath.

"Next time, I think I'll bring along a can of oxygen," Adam said. "I'm not cut out for the high-altitude life."

"Remember the governing rule when it comes to high-altitude sickness, Adam. It's not always how high you climb, but how fast. In case you didn't know, here is the common sequence of symptoms. First comes the headache, followed in turn by the nausea, the rapid heartbeat, the dizziness, and the delirium."

"Speaking as a longstanding inhabitant of the flat-earth country,

I thank you for that bit of information, which I will store away in case I ever make it back to the high country."

Across the way, the abandoned cabin and their vehicles could be seen through the trees, but it was another sight that at once eclipsed it.

"Smoke!" Adam called out, pointing in the direction of Solitaire.

CHAPTER TEN

ADAM HAD HIS RENTAL HARD ON THE HEELS OF LAUREN'S FBI van as if hitched to it, as they raced toward Solitaire. Up ahead, a plume of flames could be seen shooting skyward from within the column of smoke rising overhead.

The two pulled their vehicles to a stop aside each other, a safe distance from the grounds of the complex. From the corner of his eye, Adam caught sight of the laborers' van disappearing around the far bend in the road, hastening toward civilization.

Lauren swung open the door of her van. She was on the radio, reporting the fire. "They're sending up a helitack crew," she informed Adam.

"Are you still on the line?" he asked.

"No, but I can get right back on...what is it?"

He retrieved from his pants pocket the license plate number of the fleeing vehicle. "Here, ask the cops to be on the lookout for this plate. It belongs to the laborers' brown van. I saw it scrambling out of here. It was headed in the direction of the interstate."

Lauren took the note. "Will do."

Meanwhile, the fire had nearly engulfed the main store.

Tongues of flames were licking through the windows and up the side of the structure clear to the roof.

Adam circled the building to assess the situation. Thankfully, the complex sat on a large enough clearing to allow the helitack crew to land at a safe distance from the conflagration. The wind was very light, which worked against the fire spreading to the surrounding forest, despite the random embers that were shooting upward through the billowing smoke. Most landed on empty ground. What worried Adam were the two sheds to the rear of the main structure. Both were in danger of an advancing ground fire emanating from the back of the store. Adam figured it was caused by a flammable liquid of some sort whose containers had been ruptured by the blaze.

"Have you got a tow rope in that van of yours?" he called out to Lauren, who was hurriedly exiting the vehicle, following her radio calls.

"As a matter of fact, I do," she yelled back over the crackling flames.

"There are two sheds in the back of the store that are in the path of a ground fire coming from the main complex," he said in a raised voice. "The sheds are close to the trees. There's also a large pile of logs stacked against one of them. I'm afraid if they catch fire, the flames will spread to the tall timber."

"What do you have in mind?" she asked.

"There are rain barrels positioned next to each of the sheds. They sit atop wooden platforms. If we can pull the legs out from under them, the spill might be sufficient enough to at least slow the ground fire until the helitack crew gets here."

"Let's do it," she said, reaching into the back of her van to retrieve the tow line. "It's about twenty-five feet long. Is that enough?"

"Should be," he answered. "Circle around to the back of the store. I'll meet you there."

"Why don't you jump in with me," she said through a grin, "or do you need the exercise?"

Feeling like a fool for being oblivious to the obvious, he joined her.

She circled to the back, parking alongside one of the sheds. Adam hopped out of the van with the tow rope in hand. He tied it around a leg of the platform and to the hitch knob on the back of the van. He felt the heat of the blaze as it reached its full fury. The sound of it was akin to a giant blowtorch set on full blast.

"How much water is in these barrels...do you have any idea?" she called out through the van's front window.

"I have no idea...you tell me...how much rainfall have you had around here recently?"

"We've had some good rains in recent weeks. I don't know about up here, though."

"Okay, let's see what's in there," he said, stepping out of the way. "Go slow. It shouldn't take much to topple it. The support legs are not much thicker than stilts."

Lauren eased the van ahead, tightening the tow line before initiating the pull. At once, the leg gave way. For a few moments, the remaining three legs held fast, but then buckled under the weight. As the platform gave way, the barrel tumbled to the ground. Water gushed from it, nearly a barrel full by Adam's estimate, spreading across the nearby grounds and dousing a sizable swath of the turf fire.

Adam untied the tow line from the broken support leg. "Next one," he yelled out.

Lauren maneuvered the van to the twin shed and the process was repeated with the same result—a dousing of a substantial portion of the ground fire. Once finished with the rain barrels, Adam ran to the well.

"There's a bucket here. I'm going to toss some water around the perimeter of the fire to help slow it," he called to her.

"I'll be back to help you, but first I'm taking the van out front to get it out of harm's way."

Adam lowered the bucket into the well and filled it to the brim, first emptying it on random embers that had fallen onto the property. The conflagration had reached its zenith. He heard several loud pops and looked up to see the light stands atop the structure collapse into the inferno. Glowing cinders were now being hurled into the air with greater frequency, most still landing within the clearing and not on the forest floor or trees, thanks to the absence of wind.

He was on his fourth bucket run when he became aware Lauren had yet to return. "Lauren!" he shouted above the raging flames consuming the store. He emptied the bucket and jogged around to the front, only to be confronted by a sight that at once took his mind completely off the conflagration.

Lauren stood facing her van from the passenger side. Behind her was a man with one arm wrapped around her neck in a chokehold. With his other arm, he held her own gun against her temple. It was Cruel.

"Well, if it isn't my good buddy from this morning," the sniper crowed. "Welcome to payback time, or happy hour, as I like to call it."

Lauren had both of her hands gripping Cruel's forearm locked around her neck and her chin tucked down to relieve the pressure on her throat, already partially constricted by the drifting smoke.

Adam studied the predicament for a moment. "Why don't you replace her with me?" he asked, mustering up as much calmness as he could, knowing full well the suggestion was likely to fall on deaf ears.

Cruel hurled one of his lacerating laughs his way. "Oh, I'm not about to do anything to ease your mind, buddy, or have you forgotten what happened this morning up in those hills. I sure as hell haven't. No...what I want you to do is keep your eyes on this pretty face of hers, so I can watch you the moment it turns not so pretty."

There was no doubt in Adam's mind the guy would pull the trigger. The only thing holding him back was the perverse pleasure he was experiencing from the episode. For sure, his euphoria was about to reach its climax at any moment. He was hoping Lauren would not try to elbow the guy in the groin area, as is often taught in self-defense classes. The tactic rarely works in real life, especially when the attacker possesses superior strength. More than likely, it will enrage him more, increasing the likelihood he will carry out his threat.

"Where's that stupid mutt of yours?"

"In recovery."

"I winged him good, didn't I?"

"If I recall right, he got the best of you," Adam wanted to say, but didn't.

Lauren was squirming her body in a reflexive manner, not to break the choke hold on her, Adam realized, but to inch both her and her attacker closer to the van. He knew what she had in mind. What she needed was a distraction to help her execute it.

"Is that any way to treat a lady who has that handsome bolt-action rifle of yours laying in the back of her van?" Adam dared to ask. "Now that's a trade she might want to make—her freedom for your rifle."

Cruel glared back at him, hesitant to respond, as though weighing the truth of what he said—not about the trade but whether the rifle was actually there.

"Yep...the very same rifle you were using to take pot shots at me and the dog," he added, nudging him a little further toward distraction. "Also, hard evidence to your involvement in the slaying of Jeb Lanigan, for sure. Perhaps the only evidence."

Adam hoped to high heaven the guy would not recall the pocket calendar he had left in his off-road vehicle, or the reference to the "only evidence" would be a missed effort at persuading him of the value of the rifle to both of them.

"That's why you and I are such good buddies. We think alike," Cruel responded, leaning his head forward to glance through the van's side windows for a glimpse of the weapon. It was all Lauren needed. In a nanosecond, she leaned her back into Cruel's upper torso, raised her legs, and rammed them into the side of the vehicle, using it as a springboard to send her and her assailant flying backward and onto their backs. Before Cruel could collect himself, Lauren was on her feet, jamming one foot down on his gun hand, pinning it to the ground so she could wrest the weapon from his hand and turn it on him.

Adam rushed to her side, surveying the scene. "You put a dent in the door," he joshed. "You'll have some explaining to do to your boss."

"Believe me, that will be the number one item of interest to him after reading my report," she asserted. "Adam, there is a set of handcuffs in the glove compartment. Can you grab them and place them on this guy?" she asked while continuing to aim her pistol at the captive who all of a sudden had gone silent, probably as a result of what he perceived as an embarrassing beat-down by a woman.

Adam retrieved the cuffs and placed them on Cruel, locking his arms around a sturdy, low hanging branch of a nearby tree. "No funny stuff...I still have plenty of that bear spray left," he warned him, patting his pants side pocket.

From above came the chuff-chuff-chuff of the helitack. It descended on a direct vertical line, landing feather soft on the roadway, a safe distance from the fire. Several crew members jumped from the aircraft, one of whom approached Lauren. "Is there a water source close by?" he hurriedly asked. "There's a well in the back," she informed him.

In rapid order, the firefighters had all of their ground equipment in operation, and soon had the fire contained. By then, another FBI van was making its way onto the property.

"It's Jeff with another agent," Lauren pointed out, as they pulled up beside them.

Jeff rolled down his window. "Everything under control?" he asked of Lauren.

"More so than what it was a while back," she replied.

"Who's the guy hooked to the tree?"

"The sniper who was taking pot shots at Adam this morning."

"Oh, yeah?"

"Can you haul him back and put him on hold?"

"Sure...my pleasure."

Adam tossed him the key to the cuffs. "Handle with care."

"Incidentally, sheriff's deputies chased down those guys in the van," Jeff announced.

"How many of them were in it?" Adam asked.

"Three...two laborers and Walt, the guy who waited on us in there," he said, nodding to what was left of the burning structure.

"Were they hauling crack?" Lauren asked.

"Yes, they were. Nine jars of it."

"Are they talking?" she asked.

"From what I was told, they are being very uncooperative...for now."

"Thanks, Jeff. I'll see you in the morning."

"Interesting, they had the coke on board," she said. "Not enough time to dump it somewhere, I suppose. Hurling it out the windows would be like tossing away bundles of cash to them."

"They could have left it inside the store," Adam suggested. "Better that, than get caught with it...but, yeah, they weren't expecting anyone to arrive this soon."

"Well, they could have expected it, if Walt would have noticed which way we were headed when we left Solitaire," Lauren pointed out. "By heading in the direction of the cabin, he should have known we would have had to pass this way again on our way back to town."

"Like I mentioned earlier, crooks do get careless, which appears to be the case with this bunch. No wonder the professor wanted to know every move they made."

Jeff and his partner unhooked Cruel from the tree, re-hooked him, and walked him to their van.

"The fire inspectors should be up here first thing in the morning to check for the cause," Lauren said.

"I think we know who caused it and why," Adam responded. "*How* is only a formality."

"You know what?" Lauren said with verve. "I detect the odor of roasted peanuts."

The image of Cruel sitting atop a barrel of peanuts immediately came to Adam's mind. "So?"

"I'm hungry."

"We haven't been doing much eating today if I recall right," Adam joshed.

"There's this 24-hour diner located directly across the street from our office. How about a late-night snack, like a waffle and coffee?" she proposed. "I'll buy."

"Can't turn down an offer like that...you lead the way."

————

THE DINER WAS CALLED The Diner. Some enterprising person had taken an old train car and transformed it into one. There was room for fifteen or so booths, only two of which were occupied. "Too late for dinner...too early for breakfast," Adam opined.

They ordered coffee and the waffles, hers with strawberries and cream, his with just the cream.

"What you did today was very admirable, Lauren," he said. "I think there is much more than a little trooper in you. I don't know of many people who can maintain a calm demeanor with a gun pointed to their temple."

"Please don't ask how he got the drop on me, Adam. I don't want to embarrass myself."

"Okay, I won't ask."

She took a sip of coffee and let out a pronounced sigh. "I don't mind telling you that I was afraid...very afraid," she confessed. "You definitely helped me with your calmness, not to mention that bit of diversion you came up with."

"But I wasn't the one with the gun to my head," he pointedly replied. "Tell me...where did you learn that move to break a neck hold?"

"I was taught it by Jim Alexander at the Academy."

"I'll have to commend him for that."

"I don't think I'm betraying any confidences by telling you Jim and I once dated."

"Is that so? Nothing came of it?"

She shook her head. "No, we were both wrapped up in starting our careers at the time and ended up nearly a continent away from each other...me here and he in Tampa. We stayed in contact for a while, but the distance between us gradually took a toll and our relationship faded."

"Based on my past experience, long-distance relationships are difficult to maintain. I read somewhere that the odds are about fifty to one for there to be a successful outcome in those situations. That's not to say it can't happen," he hastily added. "The Bureau wouldn't assign you to the same office?"

"After graduation, you're assigned to a field or satellite office, according to the needs of the Bureau."

"Too bad for Jim."

"Do you know by chance if he's married?" she asked apprehensively.

"You know...I'm not sure. Are you interested in reconnecting with him?"

She shrugged in a positive manner, signaling she would welcome it. "A good man is hard to find, Adam."

"The title of one of my favorite short stories," he replied.

"You're a Flannery O'Connor fan?" she asked with pleasant surprise.

"She wields a wicked pen."

"Especially towards men, the kind I like to stay away from...in my private life, of course. The job, as you know, often demands otherwise."

"How did you end up in the FBI?"

"I guess you could say it was a family tradition that got me here. My father was an agent, as was an uncle of mine."

She glanced at his ring finger. "Married?"

"Yes."

"Not surprising. She like you?" she asked, downing a sip of coffee.

"Does she like me? I sure hope so," he cracked.

"No...no...no," she responded, waving her words away. "I mean is she like you...you know...similar traits."

He smiled at her reaction. "Oh, so is she *like* me, you mean. Let me put it this way. There is no one else like her."

She smiled and nodded her understanding. "How did the two of you meet?"

"We met on the job. Actually, she was signed on by me as my replacement. At the time, I had been working as the office manager for Pete Peterson's Private Investigations. When Pete retired, I purchased the business from him. Not long after, I hired my future wife as office manager."

"How many candidates did you interview?"

Adam looked to the ceiling, as though he had to do some serious recollecting to come up with the exact total. "One," he said impishly when finished with his feigned looking back. "She had the right answer to every question, like a student who has obtained a copy of a final exam before it is administered, except in this case the questions were all spontaneous, as were the answers."

"So, it was an office romance that led to your marriage."

"Yes, but a very slow developing one...definitely, not one from the start."

"Children?"

"One...an adopted daughter whom I also met on the job. I met her in Colorado Springs, Colorado, when I got lost in a blizzard on my way to spend a week with a former Air Force buddy. I ended up at her home. She was alone, waiting for her mother to come back from a walk, and much to my surprise and chagrin, she let me in the house. She said she was a good judge of character," Adam smiled justifiably. "The log fire in their living room was going out, so I went out to a shed in the back of the house to fetch some firewood and in doing so discovered her mom hanging from a noose. I ended up working in cooperation with the local police there on what turned out to be a homicide. She was seven years old when her estranged father killed her mother in a fit of rage, leaving her orphaned. She's now a teenager...a spirited one to say the least."

"So, you have spent some time in the high country," she teased.

"A little...very little," he confessed, "especially when footing it. Driving through mountains better suits me."

She laughed quietly. "What luck for her that you turned up that night!" Lauren exclaimed. "How old is she now?"

"She's now 16. As a matter of fact, on my return to Tampa, my wife and I plan to take her to tour some college campuses, even though she's not due to graduate from high school for a couple of years yet."

They lapsed into silence as Adam reminisced about his first encounter with Noelle and Lauren reimagined the scene. "You seem to travel a lot for a private investigator," she said at last. "Is it standard procedure for you to work the field, while your wife takes care of the office back home?"

"In most cases, yes, though there are exceptions. Her great strength is in conducting research, particularly the online kind. She has a way of sifting through the information overload to pick out that which is relevant to the case. Passing along misinformation is a grievous sin to her."

"It's good you have someone on board who's wise to the ways of the Internet," she said. "The scams are rising as fast as the usage. The elderly citizens are especially vulnerable. I had a distressed senior come into my office last week unannounced..."

"The Bureau has walk-ins?" he interrupted in a lighthearted way.

"Oh, yes...more than you might realize, though many of them we end up referring to the proper authorities. Anyway, this fellow said he received an email from a highly reputable company he had purchased a computer from a couple of years ago, as well as a maintenance contract to go with it. The email contained the date of purchase and invoice number. Accompanying the email was a photo of the company's familiar logo. They were informing him his maintenance contract was automatically renewed and that if he wished to cancel it, he should call the number they had listed. He did not want to renew it for a number of reasons, so he called the number to let them know. He then was told he had one hundred dollars coming back due to the fact he was already charged for a portion of the contract year. To facilitate matters, they would make a direct refund deposit to the bank account he had drawn on to make his payments."

"They said they would make a direct deposit to his checking account?" Adam clarified.

"Yes, and they directed him to an online program to download on his computer, one that is very legitimate by the way. It allows a group of willing participants to share a private site for purposes of a group discussion."

"He was on the phone with them all this time?" Adam interjected.

"Yes, and by virtue of his downloading the program, they had control of his computer."

"He's not seeing red flags by now?"

"Remember, he thinks he is dealing with a reputable company he has done business with in the past. Moreover, he is a novice to the advancing technology. Furthermore, he thinks he is getting money, not giving it."

"Okay, he thinks he is getting money...proceed."

"They next uploaded on his screen the procedure that would allow them to deposit the one hundred dollars into his checking account. All he had to do was type in the amount on a line where the cursor was placed. They stressed to him the importance of placing the period in the correct place. As instructed, he typed in the one hundred dollars. Moments later, the man giving directions, says, "'Mr. Smith, we regret to tell you that you forgot to put in the period, like we stressed to you.'"

"Oh, boy," Adam groaned.

"He insisted to the guy he did enter it. Suddenly, what appeared on his monitor was a shot of his bank account, the same image he would have seen if he had signed into the account himself. The information appeared current and correct, except for the balance in the account. It showed roughly thirteen thousand dollars in it, instead of the normal three thousand he kept in there. "'You see, Mr. Smith, it shows thirteen thousand dollars in your account instead of the three thousand that was there. You will need to refund us nine thousand, nine hundred back to us as soon as possible.'"

"By this time, Mr. Smith was becoming suspicious. So, without telling the caller, he jumped into his car and drove straight here. As he was telling me his story, I could hear the cellphone ringing in his pocket. 'Is that the guy on the phone?' I asked. 'Yes, it's been ringing all the way over here,' he said. 'May I answer it?' I asked. 'Yes, please,' and he handed over the phone. All I said was 'FBI, may I help you?' Well, the guy on the line went on a swearing tantrum, calling me every name in the book, and then hung up."

"Do you have any idea how they were going to get him to return the nine thousand, nine hundred bucks?"

"I spoke to one of our cyberspace crime specialists and he believed their next move was to send a follow-up email with some sort of banking code for Mr. Smith to okay that would allow them to access the account and conduct actual transactions like wire transfers."

"I thought you said they had gained access to his account?"

"That was the beauty of the scheme, Adam. They had access to his bank site displaying the account but not actual access to the account. For that, they would have needed an account number and password, neither of which they had."

"Why didn't they just ask for them in the beginning?"

"Because it would have likely scared Mr. Smith off."

"So, what Mr. Smith was seeing on his computer screen was not his real-time account but a facsimile of it showing the extra ten thousand dollars that supposedly was entered by him."

"Yes. If Mr. Smith had logged onto his bank account at any time during the exchange, it would have shown the correct three-thousand-dollar balance. Instead, he drove over here, which turned out to be a wise move on his part. Because his savings account was linked to his checking account, he could have in the end lost nearly ten thousand dollars."

"It was like they created an illusion."

"That's the point of the story, Adam. When you consider the entire catalog of crimes, many of them, if not most, start with an illusion," she opined.

"Like fake non-profit organizations," he suggested.

"You have one in mind?"

"You bet," he said.

Adam took a swig of his coffee. "Ahh! Nothing beats the diner java served in a mug."

"Agreed."

"So, I assume you've never married."

"Never married."

"Now that is surprising. Here you are, working with all of these FBI agents who are upstanding citizens and have passed thorough background checks. Surely, there are some candidates among them."

She looked at him like he was from another planet.

"Okay, what about the bad boy route? As you indicated, there are plenty of them you run into during the course of your work," he said with a wry smile.

"Like Cruel," she countered, putting an end to the line of questioning.

The waiter served them the waffles, browned to perfection. Neither wasted any time indulging themselves.

"I received a radio call on the way back verifying what Jeff said. According to the sheriff's office, Walt and the laborers are keeping their mouths shut, asking for a lawyer," she informed him. "Like many of our cases, we got into the middle of this one by request. That leaves a lot of catching up to do on our part."

"Anything I can do to help in the catching up?"

"Yes, it would be a great help to me if you could sum it all up as best you can, Adam...the whole Solitaire story...step by step...from the beginning."

"Sure, I'll give you what I know thus far. One, George Riley, the history professor, gets fired from his tenured position at Valley State College twenty years ago for missing classes due to a gambling addiction...to the game of solitaire to the bewilderment of many, including me. Two, he takes a lower-grade job at a local historical society. Three...and this is a little fuzzy, he obtains ownership of an old toll house dating back to the gold rush days for the purpose of setting up a front for a drug-trafficking operation he becomes involved in. Four, as part of the front, he sets up a fake foundation to launder the money via a general store.

Five, Jeb Lanigan appears on the scene, and my guess is, that he becomes aware of the drug trafficking. Six, Jeb is taken out before he can blow the whistle on the scheme. Seven, I'm hired by a friend of Jeb to find him. Eight, with the help of Shadow, I discover Jeb's body. Nine, Shadow and I come under rifle fire. Ten, at my direction, my office manager contacts the FBI and here we are."

"So, an addiction to solitaire, the game, is how Solitaire, the place, eventually received its name."

"You got it."

"I believe we should make a visit to the professor in the morning," she said straight out.

"I agree," Adam mumbled through a mouthful of waffle.

"I suppose we could try and track him down now on the chance he might go on the run."

"He won't," Adam said directly.

"What makes you so sure?"

"He's not the type. Pride will do that to a fellow...keep him from running...and pride is something he has in spades."

———

THE GOOD PROFESSOR was not in his office. A handwritten message was attached to his door. "Donner Party Lecture, 8:00 AM-10:00 AM," with an arrow drawn below it, pointing to a meeting room at the end of the hallway.

Lauren checked her watch. "We can wait outside until it's over, or we can catch the last portion...which is it?"

"I say we join in," Jeff said.

"Adam?"

"I'm with Jeff."

They walked to the end of the hall where the same message was attached to the meeting room door, sans the directional arrow. Lauren eased the door open, and the three entered the dimly lit room, sliding into chairs at an unoccupied rear table. Their arrival turned a few heads from the two dozen or so in attendance, including Riley's, who continued with the power-point presentation he was conducting.

"So, these are the primary lessons we've learned from the Donner Party episode," he said, ticking them off with his raised fingers. "First...those who traveled with their families survived at rates far higher than those who traveled alone. Secondly, don't be greedy to the degree you'll travel halfway across the country at unimaginable risk to reach what was, to many Americans in that era, an imagined destination. Three, have a well-thought-out plan and stick to it. Four, don't take shortcuts recommended by shady strangers along the way."

Riley shut off his machine and walked over to the light switch to brighten the room. "Let me conclude with a big 'what if' and a little, short story," he said, returning to the front of the room.

"The 'what if' has to do with James Reed, one of the leaders of the expedition, as we've learned this morning. According to Reed's daughter, her father was a friend of a young lawyer working in Springfield, Illinois at the time. His name was Abraham Lincoln... yes, that Abe Lincoln. The story is that Abe considered joining the expedition to California, but in the end, decided not to due to strong opposition from his wife."

Riley set aside his pointer, took a few steps closer to his audience, and clasped his hands together in a thoughtful pose. "Now, let's consider the 'what if'...what if Lincoln decided to join the Donner Party? Would he have provided the leadership to help overcome the many obstacles confronting the expedition? Conversely, what if he had perished, along with the others? What would that have meant for the country? Would the nation have survived the Civil War intact? Or would there have even been a Civil War in the first place, each side agreeing to go their own separate ways? Makes you wonder, doesn't it?" the professor asked.

"Now to the short story," he continued. "This one has to do with a place called Solitaire..."

The professor told the story...the fictional version of it...from its inception to its demise by fire less than twenty-four hours ago. On hearing the news, a collective groan went through the class. "I know...sad news," he said, "but when all is said and done, the building of Solitaire was a simple and respectful way of honoring the memory of that tragic expedition."

"That's terrible," an attendee said aloud from a front table. "Do they know what caused the fire?" she asked.

Riley slowly lifted his gaze to the back of the room to where the three late-arriving guests were sitting. "I'm sure investigators will learn the cause of it, shortly."

He stepped back and raised his hands like a preacher to his congregation. "Thank you all for coming. It's been a pleasure."

Several in the audience stood and clapped their appreciation, before filing out of the room with the rest, leaving the professor alone with the three remaining attendees. He walked to the back of the room to address them. "Mr. Fraley, Ms. and Mr. FBI, what brings you here—not the lecture, I presume?"

"It has to do with the last portion of your talk...the matter of Solitaire," Lauren said.

Riley scooted a chair from a neighboring table to take a seat across from them. "And what would that be?"

"We have received reports of criminal activity in the area of this place called Solitaire, including drug trafficking, a homicide, and an attempted homicide," Lauren said, taking the role of lead interrogator. "Are you aware of this?"

"There have been rumors," Riley responded, leaving it at that.

"Among the neighbors? The only one you had is no longer around," Adam was inclined to say, but held his tongue.

"You're saying you have no direct knowledge of these activities?" Lauren asked.

"Only the rumors."

"Mr. Riley, we do have evidence that you were directly involved."

"Is this the part where I ask for a lawyer?" he asked calmly.

"You have that right. Jeff, read him his rights."

So, Jeff read him his rights.

"You have the right to remain silent. Anything you say can and will be used against you in a court of law. You have the right to an attorney. If you cannot afford an attorney, one will be provided for you. Do you understand the rights I have just given you? With these rights in mind, do you wish to speak to us?"

Riley reacted to the recitation with a blank expression. "Thank you, but that was unnecessary. I waive any rights I have to an attorney. I don't need one."

Lauren continued with her questioning. "Are you familiar with a man called Cruel?"

"I am."

"Are you aware he is a suspect in the murder of Jeb Lanigan?"

"Who's Jeb Lanigan?"

Your former neighbor, you jerk! Adam screamed in silence.

"You don't know him?" Lauren continued.

"No, I don't know him."

"Have you heard of him?"

Good follow-up, Adam thought. He can't dodge that one.

"Yes, I've heard of him...from your cohort here," he said, glancing at Adam.

"So, you do know him."

"No, I don't know him. Like I said, I've only heard of him."

"Does Cruel work for you?"

"No."

"Does he patronize Solitaire?"

"On occasion."

"For what?"

"For company, for chewing gum, for peanuts, for whatever...you see, Ms....what's your name?"

"Lauren Staley...and this is agent Jeff Conley, and this is Adam Fraley, whom I believe you know."

"You see, Ms. Staley, Solitaire is open to the public in the same way a public library is, even though we may offer a vastly different product. We get all sorts of people who come in for all sorts of reasons—from those who just want to hang out, to those who want to purchase a product, to those asking for directions, to those who are looking for missing persons. Like public libraries, we also get our share of the mentally disabled, some of whom can be described as mentally disturbed."

"You're referring to Cruel?"

"You could lump him into that category, wouldn't you say so, Mr. Fraley? I'm told you have met him."

"I guess you could say our introduction was a cordial one when compared to later encounters," Adam opined.

"Mr. Cruel carried with him a pocket calendar," Lauren continued. "In the calendar, he made several notes relating to a professor. Would that be you?"

"What sorts of notes?"

"Travel expenses...check with the professor. Nosy stranger... check with the professor. Feral pigs...check with the professor," Lauren recited off the top of her head. "Those sorts of notes."

A cynical smile crossed Riley's face. "There have been a few occasions when we have asked Cruel if he could make a run into town to pick up some supplies. Regarding the feral pigs, they are a major problem in the foothills. That's been all over the news. He brought to my attention that they were scavenging on the property. Regarding the nosy stranger, I believe Mr. Fraley can answer that one for you."

Lauren and Jeff turned to Adam. "I confess. I was likely the nosy stranger Cruel was referring to."

"Did he ever confer with you on hollowed-out trees?" Jeff asked.

"Not that I can recall."

"There was a jar of cocaine found on the store shelves, labeled as laundry detergent. Are you aware of that?" Jeff followed.

Riley laughed out loud. "Do you realize how many unauthorized products are placed on American grocery store shelves every day, from live snakes to church bazaar announcements, to poison-laced medicines or foods? Sure, one unauthorized, mislabeled jar of cocaine placed on a shelf, probably as a joke, is cause for a conviction of store operators. Give me a break."

This guy is on a roll, Adam mused.

"So, you gave no orders or have any first-hand knowledge in

regard to any of these activities, including the shootings," Lauren stated.

"Let me explain something to you, if I may. I am foremost a professor, an overseer of a non-profit agency that seeks to do good in the memory of a tragic event in our country's history. I am not a puppet master. My approach to the staff is to educate them on the right way of doing things, not to give orders. I like to delegate. I explain to them the courses of action available to them and the likely consequences of each. I then rely on their judgments as to which course to take. In that regard, I would like to ask you...how did you people become experts on Solitaire in less than a week's time? What is most egregious is that you erroneously seem to think Cruel is a hired hand of mine, incapable of going his own crazed way without my influence."

Okay, Lauren, your time to shine. Jeff and I are now along for the ride.

"Oh, but Cruel is definitely at the center of this, just like you are, Mr. Riley." She firmly responded. "And it didn't take a week's time for us to figure that out. Last evening, driving home from the Solitaire fire, I called Jeff here to ask him if he could try and trace the history of Cruel's bolt-action rifle that we confiscated with Adam's help. Jeff contacted outdoor sporting supply stores in this region and, what do you know? The rifle was purchased from Jack's Outdoor Sporting Goods store three weeks ago. The interesting part is that it wasn't purchased by Cruel, though his fingerprints ended up all over it. No, it was purchased by you, Mr. Riley...with cash. Why didn't you let Cruel purchase it? Because he would never have passed a background check. Jeff checked the store's video system and sure enough, there you were on camera, buying the weapon. The date and time on the receipt that Adam found in the glove box of Cruel's vehicle matched up perfectly with the video. Solitaire does not carry weapons, nor are you a recreational hunter. You wanted someone else to do the hunting for you...the hunting of Jeb Lanigan and Adam Fraley. As for the laughable idea...as you say...of a single jar of fake laundry detergent appearing on your shelves, the subsequent discovery of nine additional jars of the so-called detergent in the possession of your staff puts the lie to your observation that it was nothing more than a bad joke." Lauren folded her arms and leaned back in her chair. "All of the above, Mr. Riley, is on the table and we haven't even begun the checking of the Hasting's Foundation's financial records."

Checkmate.

"The courts are more lenient to those who cooperate, Mr. Riley," she followed.

The professor sat quietly, looking very much like a man who wished he had never taken up that cursed card game he became addicted to long ago.

"I'm all yours, Ms. Staley," he said, resigned to his fate.

CHAPTER ELEVEN

ADAM SPENT MOST OF HIS FINAL HOURS IN RENO GIVING depositions and being briefed by the FBI. Lauren let him know there was little chance he would be required to return for a court appearance, since Riley was expected to plead guilty, pressuring all of his cohorts to do likewise in light of the overwhelming evidence against them.

"Hopefully, we can obtain from the defendants clues to the source of the drugs," she said. On the chance he would be back, he reminded her it would be his turn to treat her to a waffle at The Diner.

"By the way, I received a call from Jim Alexander this morning," she said in a cheerful manner. "I can tell you there's no longer any need of outside help to reconnect us. Your case did it."

"Are those wedding bells I'm hearing in the distance?"

The thought brought a smile to her face. "Who knows, Adam, this could be one of those long-distance relationships that does beat the fifty-to-one odds."

"Hey, I'll take that bet," he said. "Knowing Jim and now knowing you, it's a winner."

He called his client Cal Taylor to notify him of Jeb's death and the circumstances surrounding it. Taylor assured him he would take care of all his friend's personal business and inform his grandmother of her grandson's death. If she wanted to bring Jeb's estranged parents into the planning, that was up to her. He also would see to it that Jeb received a proper service, in line with his family's wishes.

Adam made one last call to Ned Garland of the Reno Beacon before leaving town to tip him off about George Riley's arrest. One good turn deserved another, he reckoned.

On his long flight back, Adam spent a considerable amount of time peering out the window at the vast expanse of land below, the same expanse traversed long ago by the Donner Party on their grueling westward journey. As Professor George Riley might have stated in one of his more truthful moments, "The Donner Party story is an excellent example of ordinary people engaged in extraordinary events...a microcosm of the story of America."

———

HE WALKED from his parking slot to his office entrance and through it. His wife's head was hidden behind her computer. His daughter was in the back of the office, picking through a file drawer.

"Well, don't everyone jump for joy at once," he cracked.

Tamra peaked from behind the computer screen. "Sorry, honey," she said and rose to give him a hug.

"Hi, Dad!" Noelle called from the back.

"What's next on the agenda?" he asked his wife.

"There are three cases pending. The files are on your desk. Take your pick."

Adam sifted through the three folders...an insurance fraud case, a cheating spouse matter, and another missing person case.

As he continued to peruse, he noticed from the corner of his eye his wife trying to gain his attention, silently mouthing something to him while nodding in Noelle's direction. "Did you bring back a present?" she finally whispered aloud in frustration.

"Mother, he's not required to bring me back a present," Noelle said, overhearing the remark.

"Oh, for God's sake, I forgot it," he blurted out.

"You forgot it?" his wife said in disbelief.

"Hold on," he replied, "I mean I forgot to bring it in. It's in the car. Let me go fetch it."

He was back in a trice, pulling open the office front door and stepping aside to let a beautiful black lab dash through it, prompting a shriek from his daughter. At first, the lab skidded on the tile floor but quickly regained his footing to speed down the center aisle to her, as she bent on one knee, beckoning him to come to her. "Oh. I love him! What's his name?"

"Shadow."

As the canine feverishly smothered his daughter's face with slobbering kisses, he turned to his wife who was, in turn, flashing him that *you didn't* look.

"What can I say? It's all been worked out. He's now a part of the family...forever."

POSTSCRIPT

CAL TAYLOR GLANCED AT THE HANDWRITTEN MAP THAT LAUREN Staley had drawn for him. He then swung his Chevy van onto the road that the map indicated would lead him to Solitaire. He rolled down his windows. It was a crisp, clear day, with an early scent of autumn filling the air.

The signboard announcing Solitaire was still standing. He parked alongside it, stuffed the map into a tote bag he had brought along, and strode toward the burned-out main structure. The refreshing scent of autumn was immediately replaced by the pungent odor of smoke lingering in the atmosphere.

He slowly circled the complex. The two sheds in the back Lauren described were also still intact. The toppled light stands rested atop the caved-in roof and collapsed walls. "A little bit of history burned to the ground," he whispered into the brisk breeze coming off the hills.

From Solitaire, he drove to the rock cabin. "There's not much to see there," Lauren had said. She was right, except for the dream of a friend, represented by every stone and ounce of sweat that went into its construction.

He was familiar with the ways people tried to fill the void left by the passing of a close friend—visiting their old hangout—cooking their favorite meal—rooting for their favorite team—watching their favorite film. The question left for him was how do you honor the dream of a friend to be left alone?

He left the grounds of the cabin on foot, crossed the trail, and commenced his hike up the hill. Nearing the top, he took from the tote bag Lauren's map on which she pinpointed the location of the hollowed-out oak tree where Jeb was found. In short order, he came upon the tree. It had been cleaned out and restored to its original state. He lingered a while, taking in the bucolic scene when he spotted next to another large oak what looked to be a good-sized snake half-hidden in the grass. He inched his way toward the object to verify exactly what it was he was seeing. It turned out not to be a snake, but an item similar to a belt. He gingerly picked it up. No, it wasn't a belt. It was a dog collar attached to a leash. Inscribed on the collar were Shadow's name and Jeb's old home address. At first, he considered holding on to it as a keepsake, but decided he would give it to Lauren, in case she needed one more bit of evidence.

He placed the collar and leash in his tote bag and pulled from it an urn he was carrying. He opened the container and spread the ashes across the hillside. Thereupon, he paused to pay his last respects, before heading back down the hill to the stone cabin and his van. Shortly thereafter, he was back on the road to civilization, feeling his better self for having traveled his good friend's final path.

———

Don't miss out on your next favorite book!

Join the Melange Books mailing list at
www.melange-books.com/mail.html

THANK YOU FOR READING

Did you enjoy this book?

We invite you to leave a review at the website of your choice, such as Goodreads, Amazon, Barnes & Noble, etc.

DID YOU KNOW THAT LEAVING A REVIEW...

- Helps other readers find books they may enjoy.
- Gives you a chance to let your voice be heard.
- Gives authors recognition for their hard work.
- Doesn't have to be long. A sentence or two about why you liked the book will do.

ABOUT THE AUTHOR

Henry Hoffman is a former newspaper editor and public library director whose works have appeared in a variety of literary and trade publications, including the Library Journal, the Midwesterner, Encyclopedia of Library Science, America: History and Life, Historical Abstracts of the United States, the Cyclopedia of Literary Places, and the Encyclopedia of Natural Disasters. He is the author of five previous novels, including Bridge to Oblivion and The Veiled Lagoon, the first two entries in the  Adam Fraley mystery series. He is the recipient of the Florida Publishers Association's Gold Medal Award for Florida Fiction.

www.henryhoffman.net

ALSO BY HENRY HOFFMAN

with Melange Books

Adam Fraley Mysteries

On A Midnight Clear

The Ephemeral File

The Perpetual Penitent

Two For the Road